Nora Barnacle Joyce

Nora Barnacle Joyce

Nora Barnacle Joyce

A Portrait

Padraic O Laoi

First published, June 1982.
Kennys Bookshops and Art Galleries Ltd.
High Street,
Galway.

ISBN No.   Standard Edition   0 906312 23X.
           Limited Edition   0 906312 24 8.

Printed by: Emerald Printers Ltd. Galway.

To Dr. Tom Wall who instigated this book.

CONTENTS

PREFACE

There is no knowing what James Joyce was thinking as he walked down Nassau Street on the 10th of June 1904. At the same time, Nora Barnacle, a chamber maid in Finn's Hotel was walking up Nassau Street possibly watching the fashion or, as they say in her native Galway, the talent.

The two met. You could have bet the Bank of Ireland against an orange that this casual meeting would never blossom into a permanent and loving relationship until death did them part. Not only did it become a total relationship, but the subsequent tryst was to carve out for itself a unique and hallowed place in the world's literature.

It is hard to explain how such an unlooked for meeting would lead to a permanent union and total dedication of two people. Nora Barnacle was by nature a warm person. She had great personal charm. She had exceptional feminine qualities which in many ways complimented Joyce's undoubted talent, and to which he responded positively as she did to him.

Nora Barnacle was a woman of great compassion. She was loyal and her trust and commitment were total. She accepted and trusted Joyce, and one can only guess at the reason why. There must have been some "inner feeling" which compelled her to take Joyce for what he was when they met on that fateful day.

Throughout the next thirty six years Nora's understanding, loyalty and compassion were to be severely tested but were never found wanting. She was to show great spirit and independence but also great tenderness and love at all times of crisis. She never lost a basic commonsense that helped her to evaluate quickly what was important and essential and reject what was not. Neither did she ever lose touch with her native Galway or her cultural background.

Nora Barnacle was an essential part of Joyce's art. She was his model for Molly Bloom, for Gretta Conroy in *The Dead*, for Bertha Rowan in *Exiles* and the day of their first date was to become Bloomsday and the setting of Joyce's novel

i

Ulysses. In the days of Joyce's abject poverty and many illnesses, of his depressions and anxieties, she sustained and

nursed him with dedication and courage that was to make them inseparable.

It is, indeed, sad to reflect that the Barnacle family which for almost two centuries added lustre to the city of Galway is no longer found there. Taking the telephone directory as our yardstick, we find the name is no longer listed for Ireland. A minor branch of the family named Barnicle is found three times.

I wish to express my sincere thanks to the many people who helped me in compiling this work: to my lifelong friend Dr. Thomas Wall who prompted and cajoled me to write this:

to Dr. Richard Ellmann for his generous help and valued criticisms:

to Kathleen Mulkerrins of the Co. Galway Records Office, Prospect Hill, for her kindness and help in researching the Barnacle records:

To "Leo" (Nora) Byrnes, Oughterard, for giving me her memories of Thomas Barnacle, Nora's father.

To Joe Butler of St. Nicholas Avenue, Galway for sharing with me memories of his visits to Galway Workhouse around 1900.

To Bridget Lydon, Waterlane, Galway for information about Galway dances and amusements.

To Mrs. Donnellan, Bowling Green, for information on the Barnacle family and Nora's last visit to Galway.

To the late Margaret Moore, Shropshire and St. Patrick's Avenue, Galway, who was also a personal friend of the Barnacles.

To the late Hetty Mulvagh of St. Mary's Street for sharing with me her memories of Nora and her brother Willie.

To the Presentation sisters Galway who heard the older sisters talk of Nora, always kindly.

To the late Anthony Conboy, St. Bridget's Tce., Bohermore for leading me to the discovery of Willie Mulvagh.

To Desmond Kenny of Kennys Bookshops for supporting me so kindly in my efforts to unearth the truth.
To Sean O Mordha, R.T.E. for his valuable information about Nora's life in Zurich.
To the Society of Authors, 84 Drayton Gardens, London as the Literary Representatives of the Estate of James Joyce .
To Seamus Cashman, Wolfhound Press, Dublin, for information on the Joyces in Europe.
To Alf McLochlain, Librarian, U.C.G. for his kind and generous help.
To Dr. Riana O'Dwyer, Circular Road, Tuam, for reading the typescript and several valuable suggestions.
To the National Library of Ireland for the use of photographs.
To the sisters of the Convent of Mercy for their generous help.

–Padraic O Laoi.

CHAPTER 1

THE BARNACLES OF GALWAY

Galway City is now proud to be referred to as the 'City of the Tribes'. It is a name first used by Cromwell's Army in 1651 as a term of reproach against the natives of the city when they invaded and pillaged it. The soldiers found the city very united and close-knit and, even in its great distress, full of care and concern for one another.

The tribes were the leading families. They were the merchants and traders of the city and they were very happy to adopt as a title of honour the insult hurled at them by Cromwell's Army. The tribes numbered fourteen in all namely Athy, Blake, Bodkin, Browne, Deane, Darcy, Ffont, Ffrench, Lynch, Joyce, Kirwan, Martin, Morriss and Skerritt.

In the course of time the tribes prospered and then migrated and emigrated. To-day the name Athy is not to be found in Galway, the name Bodkin has almost disappeared from the city as has that of Deane, Ffont, Ffrench and Skerrett. The other names remain only in scattered spots in the city and are gradually fading from its history. Yet on festive occasions in the city all the tribes are honoured by the unfurling of their Coats of Arms and Crests on the fourteen flagpoles in the centre of the city in Eyre Square: a generous tribute to the families of old.

Side by side with the tribes, Galway can boast of many other families equally ancient and respectable and who added to its lustre. One was the Barnacle family. The baptismal registers of St. Nicholas Parish, Galway city begin in the year 1798. They record the names of the child baptised, its parents and sponsors. They also record the stole fee paid by the parents to the priest on the occasion of the baptism. The amount paid is an indication of the financial and social status of the family.

In the baptismal list of August 1810 fifteen babies were baptised. Two families were so poor that they are recorded as not giving a stole fee. Seven families gave 2/6, four

1

families gave 3/4, and two gave 4/8. On 2nd August 1810 Thomas Barnacle, son of Michael Barnacle and Catherine Dempsey was baptised in the Parish Church of the city — St. Nicholas's Church. The stole fee paid was 3/4 a true indication that the family was upper middle class.

In every decade of the nineteenth century the name Barnacle is recorded in the baptismal register. We read of the baptism of Thomas White on 24th December 1827, son of Patrick White and Margaret Barnacle; his sponsors being Martin and Mary Barnacle. The stole fee paid was 2/6 which indicates that Margaret Barnacle had married beneath her. On 28th August 1829 we read of the baptism of Stephen Barnacle (how Joyce would have loved to have known of this Stephen) son of Thomas Barnacle and Margaret O'Sullivan. The stole fee again was 2/6 proving that one branch of the family was lowered from upper middle class to ordinary middle class.

The name Barnacle reoccurs in the baptismal records during the forties and fifties of the nineteenth century. When the country and city were ravaged by famines and almost wiped out by emigration the Barnacle family lived on in Galway. Indeed they were a family of substance. For instance we read in the *Galway Vindicator* of April 1867 that there was a rather stormy election meeting in Galway at the time. The election was caused by the appointment of Michael Morriss M.P. as high court judge. The candidates in the election were George Morriss of Spiddal, and Blake of Menlo. The paper reports that at the election meeting in support of Blake one of his vociferous supporters was "a Mr. Barnacle, a baker by trade".

At the same period a Nurse Barnacle was matron of the fever hospital, a building which is now the main part of University College Sport's Club. That the family, or one branch of the family, even then lived in Bowling Green is evident from an insertion in the baptismal records of 26th May 1862 that "Mrs. Barnacle, Bowling Green, was churched" ('churched' was the official name given to the church blessing given to a mother on her first appearance at church after the birth of her child). Thus the family survived the ravages of the famine years and their status in the city remained at least upper middle class.

Thus it is a travesty of the facts to say that Thomas Barnacle (father of Nora) was 'a man from God knows where', as has been suggested, or that his name was originally Coyne (Cadhain) which happens to be the Irish word for 'a barnacle goose'. Thomas Barnacle was born in Galway in 1846. He was the son of Patrick Barnacle, a baker by trade. His mother's name is not recorded in either the church or state records of his marriage in 1881.

Thomas Barnacle as a child was rather delicate and was not sent to the monastery school run in Market Street by the Patrician Brothers. So in a sense he was illiterate. But so too were more than forty per cent of the people of Galway in the 1850s and 1860s. There was no compulsion to go to school in those leisurely days and people destined for a trade as Thomas was for baking saw little use in formal education. When he reached the age of thirteen or fourteen, he was apprenticed to his father and began to learn all the techniques of plain baking and the intricacies of pastries and, at the age of nineteen he graduated as a baker.

In those days the baker had none of the permanency of job associated with the trade to-day. He was what was known as a journeyman baker. He was employed on a day to day basis and if he or his employer wanted to terminate the contract there was no difficulty from unions, as the unions were not then developed. Because he was a journeyman baker he worked in every bakery in the city. He is remembered in Griffin's Bakery in Cross Street, in Lydon's Bakery in Prospect Hill, in Lydon's Bakery in Mary Street and in bakeries in Mainguard Street and Williamsgate Street. He also worked for many years, in the period 1900 - 1912, in Jim Byrne's Bakery in Oughterard. Whenever Jim was short staffed he would go to Galway and bring out Thomas Barnacle.

Leo Byrne, daughter of Jim Byrne, who was born in 1894, and who still lives in Oughterard, remembers Tom Barnacle very well. (She in fact was christened Nora, as was her mother and grandmother before her, but her childhood coincided with the death of Pope Leo XIII, so her name was first lengthened to Leonora and then shortened to the nickname Leo.):-

"He was of medium height, about 5' 9" or 5' 10". He was thick-set, stocky and rather stout. He was very refined, a very well behaved and educated man. He was in every sense a gentleman. My father always thought very highly of him and never had the slightest hesitation in leaving us girls under his care on the occasions when my parents had to leave us to go to Galway or attend funerals or weddings. While he worked with us in Oughterard he lived in the house with us and was looked on by old and young as being one of the family. He ate his meals with us at the same table and sat with us around the fire telling ghost stories.

He had one great weakness. He was fond of drink and I often heard my father pleading with him to give up the drink. But he didn't. I don't know for sure whether he sent any money to his family in Galway, but I don't think he did. Indeed, we heard that he was separated from them. While he was working with us my sister Sarah was born. When Thomas Barnacle heard that the baby was called Sarah he chided my father and mother saying 'why did you call the baby Sarah? it is an ugly name to call a baby girl.'

While Thomas Barnacle was with us an amusing incident happened which later had its counterpart in Galway. My uncle was friendly with the daughter of a local publican and often visited her 'to chat her up'. The local sergeant of the R.I.C. was also courting this girl. The girl managed to 'two-time' the pair of suitors very successfully until the clash came.

4

My uncle was in the bar one night and his girl-friend was making a glass of punch for him when they heard the unmistakable voice of the sergeant in the hallway coming to pay court. My uncle immediately dived behind the counter hidden from the view of the sergeant. Well, the sergeant chatted his girlfriend, unaware of my uncle's presence. My uncle was very embarrassed when the sergeant began uttering intimacies and there was nothing for it but to surface and treat it all as a joke. This he did to the surprise of the Sergeant, who never suspected that he was in the presence of his rival. My uncle was a bit of a wag and soon he composed a few lines of doggerel in memory of that night

'Sweet was the punch and sweet was the maker
and under the counter was Byrnes the baker'.

Thomas Barnacle loved to tell the story of my uncle's embarrassment and to chant or hum the two lines quoted."

This episode in Oughterard was echoed in Galway at a later date. It happened one night that Thomas Barnacle when at home in Galway was drinking in Hosty's Public House in Bridge Street. He remained on after the legal closing time for public houses. Suddenly there was a rat-tat at the door. The R.I.C. police force was raiding Hosty's. To escape detection he hid himself under the counter and the following day Thomas changed the Oughterard couplet to run

'The whiskey was nice and so was the maker
and under the counter was Barnacle the baker'.

Many of the older people in the city remember with affection Thomas Barnacle. Anthony Conboy (1883-1978) was a friend of his. He thought very highly of him and considered him a man of character and uprightness who "didn't have to hide behind the door from anyone". True he took a drink but he never disgraced his family.

Annie Healy, Nora's mother, was the daughter of Patrick

Healy described in his daughter's marriage certificate as a "dealer". Her mother was Catherine Mortimer. The Healys were a family of substance in the city, who believed in education and hard work and passed on their high principles to their three children, Thomas, Michael and Annie. The three children were sent to the national schools, Annie to the Convent of Mercy and Thomas and Michael to the Patrician School in Market Street known popularly as 'the Mon'. Michael proved to be a over-average pupil and, after leaving the Mon., he continued his education at the Patrician Brothers secondary school in Nun's Island, known in Galway as 'the Bish' because it was erected by Bishop McEvilly on 12th January 1863 to counteract the proselytising influences of the Model Schools in Newcastle Road,. Bishop McEvilly named the school St. Joseph's Seminary but the name, while official, never was adopted by the people of the city and even to this day the school is known as 'the Bish'.

Michael Healy was a brilliant student. He passed all his exams with honours and was appointed to H.M. Inspector of Customs and Receiver of Wrecks, first at Galway city and later at Dublin.

Thomas Healy became a handyman. He worked as a jack of all trades but had no bother in making a good livelihood. Their sister Annie Healy attended school at the local Convent of Mercy which ever since January 1863 consisted of three separate schools, a school for the poor (free) a school for the middle class (fee to be paid) and St. Vincent's Academy for the upper class (fee to be paid). The programme of the last two included reading, writing, grammar, arithmetic, music, elocution and French.

As there were no public examinations in those days a system of examination was devised to test the students and the quality of the teaching. In the presence of the Bishop, the city priests and a large audience each child was examined orally and in depth in the various subjects and marks were allocated accordingly.

In those days the job expectation of girls was very limited.

Indeed, housework was really the only one open to them; whether they stayed at home in Ireland or emigrated to the U.S.A. or England. To meet the need of girls who wished to go 'on service' as housekeepers the nuns had in addition to the schools a workshop where girls were trained in all the chores of housekeeping; these included knitting, dressmaking and even bookbinding.

Annie Healy had a taste for dressmaking and, encouraged by the nuns, she graduated from the Mercy Convent as a dressmaker with much talent. She was much sought after in an era when clothes were not ready-made but made to measure, particularly for festive occasions such as Weddings, First Communions, and Confirmations. Thus Annie could be regarded as a girl of independent means. The Healy family lived in Whitehall which is a cul-de-sac, an extension of St. Augustine Street where that street intersects Abbeygate Street. Here Annie's mother died on 7th March 1897, a death entered in the parish records.

The state and the parish records testify that on 27th January 1881, Thomas Barnacle married Annie Healy. Thomas was aged 35 years and Annie was aged 23. Two features of the state record of the marriage are worth recalling. First, the name entered in the column stating the name of the person getting married is in the case of Annie Healy, Honoria Healy. The signature is clearly Annie Healy and there is no evidence that her baptismal name was Honoria. In the parish records it is clearly Annie Healy who is married. The second feature to be noted is that Thomas Barnacle was illiterate. He signs the state register by his mark; which takes the form of a capital X with his name filled in on either side thus:
his mark
Thomas X Barnacle.
We have already noted that illiteracy was rampant in Ireland at the time, and that Thomas, as a child, could not be subjected to the hardship of school — which began at 8 a.m. and continued through to 4 p.m. — because of his delicate condition. The stole fee paid to the parish clergy

on the occasion of the wedding of Thomas and Annie was £1.50 which was normal in those days. So the evidence here is that this was an an ordinary middle class wedding.

As was the custom then, the wedding ceremony took place in the early morning at either 7 or 8 o'clock Mass and the wedded pair reported back for work. There was a reception in the bride's home on that night where friends and neighbours gathered to join with the family on the happy occasion. At first the Barnacles lived with Mrs. Healy (Annie's mother) in Whitehall and with her brother Tom. It wasn't altogether a satisfactory arrangement and, after a few months, the Barnacle Odyssey began. They first got a room in Abbeygate Street around the corner from the Healys. Here their eldest child, Mary was born on 29th January 1882.

The Galway of the 1880s was so different from the Galway of the 1980s that it is very hard to get a full picture of it in its stark relaity. The census of 1881 gives the population of the city as 15,471. It was a city of great poverty and misery. In practically every year since 1800 it had experienced the awful horrors of hunger, disease and emigration. Year after year the call went out from the city for help and relief. The people cried out, their politicians pleaded and the priests of the city wrote heartrending accounts of the poverty and misery to the *Tablet* and the *Times* hoping thus to win sympathy. Year after year the Galway local papers carried in large bold print the one word which seemed to be the only one adequate to describe their dreadful hardships and sufferings — 'Distress'. Again and again that ugly word was headlined in the local newspapers and thrown across the House of Commons, as Galway M.P.s pleaded for help and relief. There was no escape from it except by boarding the emigrant ship and facing theuncert ainties of the voyage and life in the new world. The prospects for the unskilled workers in foreign lands were far from bright. So many were forced to stay and endure the distress in Galway on the plea that 'the devil you know is better than the devil you don't know'.

8

A factor that added greatly to the misery and distress of Galway city was its peculiar geographical situation. Its main hinterland to the north and west, consists of poor mountainy bogland completely incapable of nourishing even a fair population. It is only to the east of the city that the land is arable and fertile and so capable of feeding the city's populace. The difficulty was that this land was in the hands of absentee landlords who were indifferent to the fate of the citizens of the city.

In the nineteenth century men in Galway had very few opportunities of employment. There were no factories, no big contractors and whatever employment there was, was seasonal and temporary. The chief source of employment lay in construction — making roads, extending the docks, deepening the Corrib river bed. For those not strong enough for construction work and for those unable to get work the alternative was emigration. Thousands emigrated to the U.S.A. and to England from whence they sent money to help the family at home through the lean years. In the days when there were no state subventions, no doles and no home assistance the American or English letter was often a life saver.

In the matter of housing too, this twentieth century has seen a marvellous heartwarming change. In 1881 the luxury of owning a house was unknown except to the landlords. People lived in tenements. Several families occupied the same tenement. They entered by the same front door and like rabbits in a warren found their way to their own room or quarters. Often the room had no light, no running water, no toilet. The water had to be fetched from the nearest pump and the communal toilet was in the back yard.

In all this, Galway was no worse off than any other city in Europe. Hardship was part of the natural order of things and people tolerated a great deal more than they would to-day. The great fears were the constant threat of famine and eviction. Marriage offered little more than a life of poverty and drudgery and it was a brave man who proposed it and a braver woman who accepted its challenge.

9

Thomas Barnacle and Annie Healy pledged their troth in January 1881 and for the next twenty six years led a nomadic life in the city as they moved from tenement to tenement almost with the birth of each child. They had as issue eight children, one of whom, John Patrick, died in infancy.

Mary, the eldest was born on 29th January 1882, in Abbeygate Street. Here the family were still living - with one short sojourn near Raleigh Row, when Nora. was born on March 21st/22nd 1884. Bridget was born on 15th January 1886 in Whitehall, Margaret and Anne were born in Prospect Hill, near Eyre Square, in 1889. Thomas was born in Raleigh Row in 1891. John was born in Raleigh Row in 1894 and Kathleen was born in Newtownsmyth in 1896. Sometime after 1896 the family got a small house at 4, Bowling Green, off Market Street, and there they lived until the death of Annie Barnacle in 1940 at the advanced age of 83. This home in Bowling Green belonged to another member of the Barnacle family since 1950.

All the children were delivered at home with the exception of Nora and Kathleen. Nora Barnacle was delivered in the maternity ward of the Galway workhouse on either 21st or 22nd March 1884. The doubt about the exact date of her birth is due to the fact that whereas the state records say she was born on the 21st March, the baptismal records give her date of birth as 22nd March. This discrepancy can be accounted for if the birth took place sometime about midnight of the 21st March 1884.

The fact that Nora was born in the maternity ward in Galway workhouse need not raise any eyebrows for the Government of the day had decreed that the hospital in the workhouse must also serve as the hospital of the city of Galway. The county Infirmary in Prospect Hill was the hospital for the county of Galway. This division between Galway city and Galway county was maintained in all public Government departments. There was a county jail and a city jail, a county courthouse and a city courthouse, county M.P.s and city M.P.s.

The Galway workhouse was built in 1840 by the British Government in an effort to feed, clothe, and shelter the poor and destitute, who roamed the streets of the city or flocked into the city from surrounding districts whenever famine or pestilence stalked the land. Famine ravaged the land, not just in the years of Black Famine like 1847, 1852 and 1873, but was also known each year in the period between May and August. That was the hungry period when the fruits of the previous year ran scarce and the new crops were not yet harvested.

The workhouse was a handsome stone building. It was situated in the grounds of the present Regional Hospital approximately half-way between the main gate of Galway's Regional Hospital and the Hospital building. The main door was in the centre of the building dividing the male quarters on the right from the female on the left.

It was built to accommodate 400 inmates. But during the black years of 1847 and 1848 it was forced to house as many as 1,200. The workhouse was a refuge and home for homeless waifs and families. Here the poor, the hungry, the improverished found food and shelter. Indeed, many children were born in the workhouse, went to school there — as it had a fully equipped school — and lived out all their lives there.

There was a small hospital attached to the workhouse. Originally, it catered for the inmates but when the numbers decreased the workhouse hospital became the city hospital as well. The hospital building was situated to the rear of the main workhouse building, one drove around the main building and found a two-storied block standing apart from the main building and rather left of the centre. The visitor, who was walking, went through the main door of the work- house, straight through the building into the backyard and thus to the main door of the hospital.

Joe Butler of St. Nicholas' Avenue remembers visiting a sick uncle in this hospital in his youth. His lasting memory of these visits was the size and strength of the latch that opened and closed the door. One had to lean ones full weight on the latch to open the door it was so big and heavy. The hospital had wards and beds donated by individuals and charitable organisations. Brass plaques at the doorways and over the beds commemorated the donors, most of whom were citizens of the city, some of whom were members of the tribal clans whose homes were far away from their native city.

One story my friend remembers concerning the hospital highlights the credibility of the people at that time. It is a story in which fiction is mixed with fact. It seems that one night in the hospital ward, when all the patients were fast asleep or had fully composed themselves for the night, just on the last stroke of midnight the large latch of the entrance door was pressed down and with a squeak the door was pushed ajar and a dark figure walked through the ward and went out the back door. A few patients noticed the stranger and had a 'queer' feeling.

The following day, they spoke about it and passed it off as being a prank of some playboy. The same apparition reappeared the next night. Now, the patients were disturbed and wanted assurance and an explanation of the appearances so a plan of action was formed. It was decided that one man would question the strange man if he showed himself again.

Sure enough on the third night, right on the stroke of midnight the latch was lifted, the door squeaked and in walked the strange visitor. Jack Butler sat up in bed and with the courage born of fear and determination he addressed the stranger. "I demand to know who you are?' he shouted adding 'in the name of the Father, Son and Holy Ghost'. With that there was an unearthly shriek and out of the smoke and fire that lit up the ward was heard the one word 'Beelzebub'. Later, people offered as an explanation the fact that quite recently a sick man had committed suicide in the ward and that now his ghost was looking for peace.

Why it was necessary for Mrs. Barnacle to enter hospital on her confinement for the birth of Nora is not now known.

The fact that Nora was baptised on the day of her birth is proof that she was considered to be in danger of death and the doctor had forseen this crisis.

During part of her pregnancy the Barnacles lived in Sullivan's Lane off Raleigh Row. Indeed it was from Sullivan's Lane that Mrs. Annie Barnacle entered the Union Hospital. While Annie was in hospital, Thomas Barnacle obtained a room in Lower Abbeygate Street, near the Healy home.

In due time Mrs. Barnacle and Nora came to their home in a tenement in Lower Abbeygate Street which tradition says was beside the Browne Town House from which in 1905-6 the beautiful doorway was transferred to its present site in Eyre-Square at a cost of £55.00. An E.S.B. sub-station now occupies the site. Here she lived for only a year when the family changed to Whitehall less than fifty metres distant from where her grandmother Kate Healy (nee Mortimer) lived.

It was quite common in those days for the grandmother to 'adopt' one of her grandchildren and thus relieve the burden on the mother who had to cope with two or three young children and was expecting another baby. By June 1886 the Barnacles, with the birth of Bridget (called Dilly) had three children, and Nora was 'adopted' by her grandmother in so far as that here Nora slept and ate, without of course losing contact with her family.

It is interesting to note that Mary Barnacle, Nora's oldest sister when asked in 1953 about Nora's fosterage said her grandmother lived in Nun's Island, which lies west of the river Corrib just north of O'Brien's Bridge, on the road from the bridge to the New Cathedral. Yet it was not to Nun's Island but to St. Augustine Street that James Joyce, on the 26th August 1909 'went to where you (Nora) lived with your grandmother'.

This discrepancy between St. Augustine Street and Nun's Island can be explained in many ways. Between 1884 and 1897, the year she died, grandmother Healy may have lived in Nun's Island for some time and was visited here by her

13

granddaughter Mary Barnacle, or it may be that Kathleen Healy changed from Whitehall to Nun's Island, or it may even be that her other grandmother, Mrs. Barnacle lived in Nun's Island.

CHAPTER 2

THE YOUNG NORA

Nora Barnacle grew up in the very heart of Galway. In all the changes of homes made by her parents they never moved more than a few hundred yards from the city centre except in the years 1891-2 when they lived in Raleigh Row which lies behind the Jesuit Church on the old road from Galway to Connemara. Even Raleigh Row is less than 800 metres from Shop Street, the city centre. Nora lived in Whitehall through all the changes. When she reached the age of five she enrolled in the Convent of Mercy School at Newtownsmyth.

The Mercy sisters had first come to Galway in May, 1840 and had their first convent in Lombard Street on a site which now forms part of the school yard of St. Patrick's Boys School. They were essentially social workers, attending the poor and needy, the widows, the orphans, the magdalens. They performed heroic work in the famine years, caring for the sick and opening soup kitchens to give some sustenance to the starved people of the city.

In order to prepare the girls of the city for the world they would meet in England and America, the sisters founded a schools to educate them. They opened national schools and an industrial school and later, in 1859, a secondary school. Thus in 1889, when Nora Barnacle went to the infant school in the Convent of Mercy, she was following in the footsteps of her mother and probably her grandmother. Here she was taught, in the fashion of the age, the rudiments of the 3 Rs and possibly sewing, singing and music.

In due time, at the age of seven, Nora Barnacle with her class was prepared for First Communion. The First Communion in Galway was a momentous and emotional day for the communicants and their families. St. Nicholas's Pro Cathedral at the corner of Middle Street and Abbeygate Street was thronged for the occasion. The young boys wore soutanes and surplices (supplied by the Sisters of Mercy) and the girls wore flowing white dresses (also supplied by the Sisters of Mercy). The Sisters felt that poor parents should not be embarrassed on such a day and that all the children should at least appear equal. Before Mass, they sang the Hail Mary and the Our Father and, usually, the Bishop himself said the Mass and gave the young children Communion. After Mass, the first Communicants roamed the streets visiting the neighbours and later the relations filling their pockets and purses with gifts and presents.

Nora Barnacle attended the Convent of Mercy National School until she reached the age of thirteen. She has not been remembered in the school for any outstanding achievement. She must have been an ordinary run of the mill scholar in conduct and in the academic field because she left no memories amongst her teachers.

Yet her handwriting, as seen in her letter of 16th August 1904 to James Joyce, is full of character and discipline. It is written with clarity and confidence giving ample evidence of a sound and well-rounded schooling. Granted it was written by a young lady who is trying to impress her lover, yet the writing clearly reveals a maturity and independence which one would not expect from a national school education.

Nora must, however, have shown some exceptional qualities at school, as the Mercy Sisters recommended her for the somewhat prestigious job of portress at the Presentation Convent — then an enclosed order — a recommendation which would not have been lightly given .

Nora had a very pleasant manner. She was highly efficient and most reliable in 'running messages'. She was remembered with affection by the nuns and their visitors. She began her job as portress at the age of thirteen in 1897 and continued there until she left for Dublin in 1904.

The Presentation Order of the Blessed Virgin Mary had been founded in Ireland in Cork in 1777. In 1815 the Rev. Bartholomew Burke, one of the vicars in the city had introduced the order to Galway to promote education amongst the poor girls of the city. The nuns first occupied the old Dominican nunnery in Kirwan's Lane off Cross Street but found the premises unsuitable.

In March 1816, scarcely six months after their foundation, they moved to Eyre Square where they taught for three years. In 1819 the Charter School property in Presentation Road was offered for sale and the Presentation Sisters, aided and abetted by the warden of the city clergy Dr. Edmund Ffrench, purchased the Charter School where the convent of nuns and the schools have been situated ever since. Prior to becoming a Charter School, the building was a military barracks, a defence outpost situated on the western bank of one of the Corrib streams.

Military barracks, Charter School, and now, a Presentation Convent; the character of the building changes with the various occupants. The nuns built a surrounding wall some thirty feet away from the building sufficiently high to give defence and privacy. The entrance to the convent was through a doorway in this wall which was generally locked.

The duties of the portress were principally to answer calls at this door. The system lived on until 1960 when Pope John opened the gate of all churches and convents. You rang the outside bell and waited until the portress opened the outer door. The portress listened to your enquiry, and, if the case demanded it, she led you to the public parlour where Reverend Mother heard and dealt with your difficulty.

In the period in which Nora Barnacle worked as portress 1897-1904 the character of the Presentation Convent was quite different to what it is to-day. Then the nuns led an enclosed life. They had cut themselves away from the world and spent their lives in prayer and work, more or less as the enclosed orders of the Poor Clares and Carmelites still do. There was too a division amongst the nuns in their status and calling. In the inner sanctum were the professed sisters who had cut themselves off completely from the world. Serving the needs of the professed sisters and the general public were the lay sisters, who embraced the religious life

17

were not enclosed.

The opportunities for recreation in the Galway of 1890 were very limited compared with those of to-day. In a world which knew nothing of cinema, radio or television, people had to fashion their own recreations. Indoor there were card games and parlour games, singsongs and storytelling, musical evenings and dancing. Galway boasted of two theatres and Fr. Dooley's Temperance Hall in Lombard Street, where plays and concerts were held and, even if one could not afford the price on the entrance ticket, the performance was a major topic of conversation in the days and weeks that followed. All of Galway was therefore familiar, directly or indirectly with the plays of Shakespeare, Sheridan and Goldsmith as well as with the famous international and national singers and musicians of the day. When the assizes were held in the town hall in early May and August, the gentry flocked into town. The absentee landlords of the county lived mainly in London. Many of them had town houses in Galway. These usually came to attend the assizes where justice was dispensed and questions of finance and local government were decided by the grand jurors and members of the various boards. Such meetings caused a great stir in the city. They also brought much revelry by night. Dances or as they were called then 'balls' were spectacular features of the occasions and lasted generally all night.

1903 was a very special year in the history of the city. The home fleet of the British navy spent three full days anchored in Galway Bay at the end of March and the ratings, as they came ashore, brought much colour and excitement to the life of the city.

At the end of July, King Edward VII came on a royal visit to the city. His party came by Royal Yacht to Killary Harbour travelled by car to Recess and by train from Recess to Galway. They then drove in open cars from the Great Southern Hotel down the main street and on to the Docks to rejoin the Royal Yacht. It was a spectacle of colour and grandeur very much appreciated by the citizens of the city and by none more than the younger generation. The ordinary people of the city were only passive spectators of these spectacles but they were in their own way immersed in them all.

One carnival outing the people of the city had which was their very own was what was known as 'maying' at Menlo. It was called 'maying' for the simple reason that the carnival festivities took place on each of the four Sundays in the month of May. The festivities took place in the lawns of the Blake Castle at Menlo on the river Corrib a mile or so up stream by boat from the city or three miles for those who had to walk it or go by horsecar. The Blakes soon after the Great Famine gave a blank invitation to everyone in the city to come to their receptions on each of the four Sundays of May.

There were competitions in running, jumping, weight-throwing, swimming and rowing. There were sideshows of hitting the 'Maggie' (someone standing in a large barrel who would challenge all comes to hit him as, jack-in-the-box like, he raised and lowered his head), walking the greasy pole (a sturdy timber pole, well greased with heavy cart grease, was set up projecting over the water and contestants tried to walk right out to the end of the pole), throwing rings trying to cover any article on show in the arena.

Then, on Sunday afternoons, the young people indulged in crossroads dancing. This dancing was frowned on by both parents and clergy and so the dancers withdrew some-what from the centre of the city. The two crossroads which were favoured by the dancers were those at Nile Lodge and at Coolough Cross on the Headford Road. Here the lads and lassies gathered and danced to their hearts content. Here they made friendships and dates.

The dancing came to an end at tea-time, as all made sure that they were at home in time for tea, thus assuring their parents of the innocence of such trysts. It is on record that a priest out in Coolough approached the dancers one Sunday afternoon. When they saw him approaching, the dancers ran from the scene in case they would be recognised

19

and their parents informed. The evils of dancing was the subject of the sermon at all Masses in the city on the following Sunday.

The Barnacle family would have been observers of the gaiety of the visitors at the assizes. They would have watched from the sidewalks the comings and goings of the landlords and gentry. They would have been present when King Edward VII and his party drove through the town and would have enjoyed the spectacle of Royal splendour.

They would have dreamed the dreams of emulating them in their clothes and behaviour, yet these events were in a certain sense alien to them and in no way racy of the soil.

They were amongst their own 'maying' in the lawns of Menlo Castle where they rubbed shoulders with their own kith and kin. They drew from the wells of the past as they sat around the fire, listening to the stories of famed Galway men, who fought with the Connacht Rangers or sailed the four seas in the British Navy. The letters from America, from uncles and aunts were kept in safe-keeping behind the picture of the Sacred Heart in the kitchen and, now and then, they were taken down and re-read, recalling the family's successes and failures in far foreign lands.

Then there was the hustle and bustle of election time as the city was divided and disturbed, as the candidates canvassed and gave speeches in Eyre Square and to the congregations after Mass. In the election of February 1886, Capt. O'Shea was hoisted on the city by Parnell. But Captain O'Shea resigned his seat in early June 1886, just four months after his election, and Parnell soon had an Antrim man named Pinkerton elected as M.P. for the city.

Galway at this period was subjected to an invasion of street-preachers and proselytizers. On one occasion six preachers pitched their stand boxes in the Square and invited all and sundry to listen to the 'good news'. Charles McDonnell had five of his children spirited away and Fr. Mark Conroy warned people not to attend Dr. Bernardo's entertainment as it was nothing other than a cover for proselytizers.

All these street activities influenced the thinking of the young people maturing in Galway at the time and, no doubt, impressed many of them. Nora Barnacle had greater freedom of movement than most and so would have been present at all or some of the many diversions in the life of the city. Her grandmother Catherine Healy who was fostering Nora, died in the year 1897 when Nora was thirteen years old. From then until she left Galway in 1904 she was under the care of her uncle Thomas.

In his monumental biography *James Joyce*, Richard Ellmann gives an insight into the life Nora led during this time. This account was dictated by Mary O'Holleran Morris, Nora's closest friend in Galway, to Kathleen Barnacle, Nora's sister: —

"We were pals for years we were then only 16 years old my name was Mary O Holleran then we were always together until she went to Dublin she was working in the presentation convent then she was the straightest pal I ever had. When we used to get a penny for sweets which was very seldom in those days we would go to a Mrs. Francis she was nearly blind and had a sweet shop in Prospect Hill. While she would be looking for the half-penny weight we would have the pound weight on the scales and Nora would hold up her pinafore for the sweets and we would be away like hell with roars of laughter and our pinafores full of sweets we would go into another old woman and ask for a pennyworth of cough lozengers and pinch as much more out of the jar while her back was turned and again have a great laugh. There was a young man Jim Connell, he used to come into our house he was always waiting for his passage for America. This night Nora and I bought a card of Jelly babys they were sweet babys niggers what we call nigger babys they were black sweets we got the largest envelope we could get and sent the card of

21

nigger babys by post to Jim as Jim could not read he ran across to our house thinking he had his passage for America and when the packet was open he had 12 nigger babies we had to run and could not be seen for a week he left it on his sweetheart a girl by the name of Sarah Kavanagh from the country and he never spoke to her after that.

We had a party one Holly eve night. My father used to make games for us such as cross sticks hanging from the ceiling there would be an apple on one stick soap on the other and a lighted candle on the other stick our eyes would be covered so we could not see and my father would spin the sticks around and we would bite at the apple my father would put the soap in Noras mouth the house would be in roars of laughter while Nora would be getting the soap out of her mouth we would fill our mouths with wheat and then go round the house listening at the doors to hear if a boys name mentioned as he would be our supposed future husband and we would burst out laughing and run like the dickens for fear of the boys would catch us but they could never catch us we would then go to another house and buy a pennyworth of pins we would stick 9 pins into the red part of the apple and throw the 10th pin away we would put the apple with the pins in, in our left foot stocking and tie it with our right foot garter and put it under our head when we would go to bed to dream of our future husband we would steal a head of cabbage out of a garden we never stood in before on a moonlight night on Hallow eve and have a mirror we would go into a field and stand on a dunghill and eat the head of cabbage and looking through the mirror to see if we could see the face of our future husband. Those were the old fashioned

charms we used to play on Hallow eve."
(Ellmann,:- *James Joyce*, pp. 163-164)
Nora Barnacle was a vivacious girl full of fun and
devilment. She was very good looking, rather tallish, blessed
with beautiful auburn hair and sparkling eyes. She had a
charming personality and was excellent fun in company.
Further on in her account, Mary O'Holleran Morris describes how they would dress up in men's clothes with their
hair stuck up under their caps. They would then ramble
up the main street and around the Square, taking infinite
delight in meeting friends who did not recognize them.
They even met Nora's uncle Tommy, who was the bane of
her life one night and he did not know them.

Two shops they visited for sweets are no longer in that
business. Indeed Mrs. Francis sweet shop has long since
been demolished and the site is now incorporated in the
lounge bar room in Curran's hotel, 15 Prospect Hill. Mr.
Bodkin's sweetshop at No. 2 Prospect Hill was sold by the
family. To-day it is owned by John O'Loughlin who runs a
very successful drapery business there.

Mary O'Holleran Morris also gives a graphic description of
the romances of Nora Barnacle from 1898 to 1904. Her first
was Michael Bodkin, 2 Prospect Hill, with whom she fell
deeply in love when she was barely fifteen, and Michael
(nicknamed Sonny) was just eighteen, a student in University College, Galway.

The account given by Mary O'Holleran tallies in all
respects with the story of her life as told by Nora to James
Joyce in the days of their courtship in 1904. James tells
the story in a letter to his brother Stanislaus under the date
3rd December 1904. In this letter, Joyce fills in more
detail of Nora's family background and her early Galway
romances.

"Nora's father is a baker. They are seven in family.
Papa had a shop but drank all the buns and loaves
like a man. The mother's family are 'toney' and (by
the way, do you ever see Paddy Lee?) intervened.
Sequestration of Papa. Uncle Michael supports Mrs

23

and the children, while Papa bakes and drinks in a distant part of Connacht. Uncle Michael is very rich, Papa is treated contempuously by the family. Nora says her mother would not lie with him. Nora has not lived at home but with her grandmother who has left her some money.

She has told me something of her youth, and admits the gentle art of self-satisfaction. She has had many love-affairs, one when quite young with a boy who died. She was laid up at news of his death. Her uncles are worthy men as you shall hear. When she was sixteen a curate in Galway took a liking to her: tea at the presbytery, little chats, familiarity. He was a nice young man with black curly hairs on his head. One night at tea he took her on his lap and said he liked her, she was a nice little girl. Then he put his hand up under her dress which was shortish. She however, I understand, broke away. Afterwards he told her to say in confession it was a man not a priest did 'that' to her. Useful difference. She used to go with Mulvey (he was a Protestant) and walk about the roads with him at time(s). Says she didn't love him and simple went to pass the time. She was opposed at home and this made her persist. Her uncle got on the track. Every night he would be at home before her. 'Well, my girl, out again with your Protestant'. Forbade her to go any more. She went. When she came home uncle was there before her. Her mother was ordered out of the room (Papa of course was away) and uncle proceeded to thrash her with a big walkingstick. She fell on the floor fainting and clinging about his knees. At this time she was nineteen ! Pretty little story, ah!"

(Letters Vol. 11, p. 72)*

It is worth examining the people mentioned in this letter in the order of their appearances. The first reference is to Nora's father. In 1904, Thomas Barnacle was 58. He had worked in every one of Galway city's bakeries, and was now working in Byrne's bakery in Oughterard. (Sarah Byrnes was born in January, 1905 and Thomas Barnacle was working there then).

There is no memory in the city of Barnacle's shop where on Nora's evidence "Papa drank all the buns and loaves like a man." Bridget Lydon of Waterlane, Bohermore, who was born about the turn of the century thought that Barnacle's bakery shop was in Williamsgate St., in premises which in the course of years changed hands many times and finally was bought by Corbetts to be incorporated in their new shop.

By way of excuse for Thomas Barnacle's drinking one is entitled to look at the life style of the journeyman baker. He entered the bakery around midnight to begin the kneading and to prepare the ovens. He worked all night until all the batches of bread were ready for despatch in the early morning.

Such a daily routine was not very conducive to leading a full family life. He came home around nine o'clock in the morning and went to bed. He arose between 4 and 5 p.m. ate his dinner, and then walked the town. It is generally acknowledged, that, because of the excessive heat generated at the ovens, bakers must consume a fair quantity of liquid. In some cases the liquid may be intoxicating and if the baker has a little weakness for intoxicants, then there is trouble brewing. On the evidence of his daughter, Nora, on the evidence of Leo Byrne, Thomas Barnacle had such a weakness. Yet Anthony Conboy rejected the idea that Tom Barnacle drank to excess. He testified that while Barnacle did take a drink, he was no better nor worse than the average drinker.

We know now that when Nora left Galway in 1904 that Thomas Barnacle was working at Byrnes bakery in Oughterard. So "the distant part of Connaught" is the town of Oughterard. Thus James Joyce may have heard for the first time from the lips of Nora Barnacle the poetic name Oughterard. He would have hidden it away in the recesses of his mind to be used in good time in the story of *The*

Dead as the burial place of Michael Furey. For in 1904 Nora Barnacle's father lay, so to speak, buried alive in Oughterard.

Thomas Barnacle was on friendly terms with his family. He was a constant visitor to the family in Bowling Green. He never lived there because the house was a two-roomed house and there was no sleeping accommodation for a man in a house which was the home of a mother and four grown-up daughters.

In the latter years of his life Thomas Barnacle lived in Mary Street, just a few hundred yards away from Bowling Green. In June 1921 he fell seriously ill. His wife Annie nursed him tenderly each day until it was decided that he should be removed to hospital. The city hospital was still the Workhouse Hospital in Newcastle Road. Here he died on the 13th July 1921. His wife made all the funeral arrangements. She purchased a grave for him in Rahoon Cemetery, and here he was buried on 14th July 1921 in Section G, Row 14, No. 5, quite near the grave of Michael Bodkin.

Referring again to Joyce's letter of 3rd December 1904 we read 'The mother's family are 'toney'." The Healy family in 1904 numbered three. Annie the wife of Thomas Barnacle and her two brothers Michael and Thomas. Michael was a civil servant in the city and was very good to his sister Annie. Every week he gave her an allowance and supported her in every way possible in her struggle to rear her family. Thomas lived in Whitehall in the family home where he looked after Nora on the death of his mother in 1897. He had a testing job and he did his best to guide and mould her. The Healys first lived in St. Patrick's Avenue, off Eyre Square and later moved to Whitehall.

As a loyal civil servant Michael Healy considered it his duty to recruit men to fight in the English side in the Great War 1914-1918. In doing so he was acting in the tradition of a city which had always fought on the side of the British. The Connacht Rangers had its home base in the city and there is scarcely a family in the old city but has a picture of

26

a member of the Connacht Rangers hanging in the kitchen. The British navy always drew a large number of ratings from the fishermen of the city.

Michael Healy's generosity extended to succouring and helping Joyce and Nora in their many cries for help. Joyce acknowledged this debt in a gracious letter to John Howley, librarian in University College, Galway, dated 29th July, 1935. The letter reads-:

"Dear Sir: My uncle-in-law Mr. Michael Healy has asked me to send you a prospectus concerning the facsimile MS. edition of my booklet *Pomes Pennyeach* (so brought out in Paris in 1932) which I had much pleasure in offering to your library and you the graciousness to accept. Two other European libraries possess copies, the Bibliotheque Nationale here and the British Museum in London. But I wished to offer a copy to your library not only because the daughter of the lettrines is a grand-daughter of your city and the writer of these verses bears one of its tribal names but also as a small acknowledgement of a great debt of gratitude to Mr. Healy himself for his kindness and courtesy during so many years."

(MS. University College, Galway).

One month later, Michael Healy sent a letter from the Obelisk Press, the publishers, to the Librarian. In the accompanying note he describes how an English auctioneer got a little mixed up in his terminology when cataloging the book:—

"Mr. Joyce has asked me to give you the enclosed letter from the Obelisk Press which explains the process of reproduction of his "Pomes Pennyeach". The paper is known as iridescent Japan. It may amuse you to know that a few days ago Mr. Joyce was informed by the publisher that a short time ago a copy of it was put up for auction in England and the show catalogue informed would be purchasers that the book was an "indecent

Japanese paper".
(MS. University College, Galway.)
Michael was a man of deep faith. When he retired from the civil service he could be found each day in the Pro Cathedral and the Abbey Church in Francis Street. He died in the Abbey while attending Mass in 1935 and lies buried in the new cemetery.

Michael Healy's brother Tommy was tall of stature and broad shouldered. He worked as a general labourer in the city and was the breadwinner for his mother until her death, and then for Nora Barnacle, his niece who lived with him in Augustine Street. He was a great walker in the tradition of a city of great walkers. People still remember him, with his blackthorn stick, whistling to himself as he strolled towards Salthill or up the Dyke Road. He was very conscious of his position *vis a vis* his niece Nora. He realised that he was acting *in loco parentis* and so was rather severe on his teenage niece in that he controlled her movements, and kept a watchful eye on her companions, and their haunts.

When Nora Barnacle got the job at the Presentation Convent it gave her a certain amount of independence from her uncle, and allowed her to meet and flirt with young men of the city. Soon she was attracted by a Michael Bodkin whose parents had a little shop at No. 2 Prospect Hill. The Bodkins were an old Galway family whose ancestors were numbered amongst "the tribes" of the city.

Michael Bodkin was the son of Patrick Bodkin, of Bushypark a few miles west of Galway city, and Winifred Pathe who came to Galway from Cork city. He had one brother, Leo, and no sisters. He was a pleasant warm-hearted boy. He was handsome with a beautiful head of black wavey hair. He had registered as a student in University College, Galway, although as a Catholic he was forbidden to attend the 'Godless College'.

This prohibition on Catholics was promulgated at the Synod of Thurles in 1850 and was strictly enforced in the cities graced with universities and in the dioceses of these cities. Outside these dioceses the prohibition was not as strictly enforced and therefore many anomalies existed in the exercise, of the law. For instance, a student who attended the university of Galway committed a reserved sin which could only be pardoned by having recourse to the Bishop of Galway or his delegate. But if the student travelled out sixteen miles to Athenry, he was in the diocese of Tuam where it was not a reserved sin to attend the 'Godless University,' and so he could easily get pardon of his sins. And so it became the practice at the time, for Catholics who attended U.C.G. in the city to seek pardon of their sins in the neighbouring dioceses of Tuam.

There is no record that Michael Bodkin ever gained a degree at the University. His death certificate records that he was a clerk and local tradition says he worked as a clerk in the Gas Company offices. He must then have abandoned his course at the University some time after he entered it, whether it was that the Catholic clergy of the parish pressurised him to do so, or he was disillusioned by university life and opted for a job that was offered we will never know now.

This Gas Company clerk, this handsome young man admired and courted the auburn-haired Nora Barnacle who, at the age of fifteen, was already blossoming into a charming lady. Nora Barnacle was very impressed by the gentility and manliness of Michael, and became very attached to him. The opportunities for courtship for teenagers were then very limited. Nora would visit the Bodkin shop at Prospect Hill and there throw eyes at Michael as they chatted and joked and passed small pleasantries. After Mass on Sundays they would meet at walks and hold hands as they raced through the fields around Terryland on the banks of the river Corrib. Or they would take the horse tram to Salthill, a holiday resort, a few miles west of the city where they would stroll along the promenade at the sea front.

Michael Bodkin was aged 18 and Nora Barnacle had just passed her fifteenth year, when he gave her a present of a bracelet. The present was not of any great value moneywise

but it was Michael's way of showing Nora that he appreciated and valued her friendship and person. Nora was very
much aware of the full significance and implication of the
giving and receiving of the bracelet, and she kept and
treasured it through the ups and downs of her later life.

But, alas, just when their love was beginning to grow into
maturity Michael was stricken with tuberculosis which was
the killer disease of the early 20th century. Michael pined
away at home, and was removed to the tuberculosis wing of
the County Infirmary for medical treatment. The treatment
was not successful and Michael Bodkin died in the Infirmary
on February 11th 1900. His death as recorded in his death
certificate was due to "valvular heart and rheumatism."

In his biography, Richard Ellmann states that Bodkin died
in the year 1903 and suggests that he was buried in Oughterard. The Church records show only one Michael Bodkin,
the Michael who died on 11th February 1900. This Michael
Bodkin lived at No. 2 Prospect Hill. He was the son of
Patrick Bodkin and Winifred Pathe. He was buried in
Rahoon Cemetry two miles north west of the city. His
tomb is in the form of a raised cubular stone vault some
four feet over the ground. The inscription may be hard to
make out, but with a little patience and rubbing one reads
'Michael Maria Bodkin, son of Patrick L. and Winifred,
died on 11th February 1900 at the age of 20.

The State files in the County Buildings Galway have no
record of the death of a second Michael Bodkin in or
around the city of Galway, or in the neighbourhood of
Oughterard, between the years 1895 and 1905.

Thus Church and State records agree that only one Michael
Bodkin died in the year 1900 and that he was buried in
Rahoon, James Joyce himself makes it clear that Michael
Bodkin is buried in Rahoon. In the 'Notes to Exiles' he
wrote:

"Moon: Shelley's grave in Rome. He is rising from
it: blond she weeps for him. He has fought in vain
for an ideal and died killed by the world. Yet he
rises. Graveyard at Rahoon by moonlight where

30

Bodkin's grave is. He lies in the grave. She sees his tomb (family vault) and weeps. The name is homely. Shelley's is strange and wild. He is dark, unrisen, killed by love and life, young. The earth holds him.
Bodkin died. Kearns died ......
Rahoon her people. She weeps over Rahoon too, over him whom her love has killed, the dark boy whom, as the earth, she embraces in death and disintegration."
(*Exiles*, Viking Press, New York 1951, pp. 117-8)
Why then is there some confusion about the date and place of burial of Michael Bodkin. It arises from different analyses of the background to James Joyce's most famous short story *The Dead*. The famous story draws from many incidents in the history of the Joyce family. Into the web of this story Joyce spun an incident in the life of Michael Bodkin and his courtship of Nora Barnacle. In the story Joyce alters many of the details. When Joyce named a person or place in *The Dead* he changed or kept the name as it suited him. He called Michael Bodkin/Michael Furey and he models Gretta on Nora Barnacle. In the story Gretta says that Michael Furey came to see her at her grandmother's house in Nun's Island. Let us look for a moment at the particular incident in *The Dead*.

"It was in the winter', she said, 'about the beginning of the winter. when I was going to leave my grandmother's and come up here to the convent. And he was ill at the time in his lodgings in Galway and wouldn't be let out, and his people in Oughterard were written to. He was in decline, they said, or something like that. I never knew rightly'.

She paused for a moment and sighed.

'Poor fellow', she said. 'He was very fond of me and he was such a gentle boy. We used to go out together, walking, you know, Gabriel, like the way they do in the country. He was going to

31

study singing only for his health. He had a very good voice, poor Michael Furey'.

'Well; and then?' asked Gabriel.

'And then when it came to the time for me to leave Galway and come up to the convent, he was much worse and I wouldn't be let see him, so I wrote him a letter saying I was going up to Dublin and would be back in the summer, and hoping he would be better then'.

She paused for a moment to get her voice under control, and then went on: 'Then the night before I left, I was in my grandmother's house in Nun's Island, packing up, and I heard gravel thrown up against the window. The window was so wet I couldn't see, so I ran downstairs as I was and slipped out the back into the garden and there was the poor fellow at the end of the garden, shivering'.

"And did you not tell him to go back?' asked Gabriel.

"I implored of him to go home at once and told him he would get his death in the rain. But he said he did not want to live. I can see his eyes as well as well! He was standing at the end of the wall where there was a tree"!

'And did he go home? asked Gabriel.

'Yes, he went home, And when I was only a week in the convent he died and he was buried in Oughterard, where his people came from. O, the day I heard that, that he was dead !.'

What happens in a story is not expected to follow all of the details of the incident that suggested the story. We know that Joyce has changed many of the facts on which *The Dead* is based. Nora worked in a convent in Galway, not in Dublin. When she went to Dublin Michael Bodkin was already four years dead. And her boyfriend in Galway in 1904 at the time of her departure for Dublin was Willie Mulvagh (Mulvey) not Michael Furey.

Further, I have failed to find any evidence that Nora Barnacle's maternal grandmother, Mrs. Healy, ever lived at Nun's Island, although her paternal grandmother, Mrs. Barnacle may have lived there. Nun's Island is an island on the river Corrib adjacent to Galway's majestic Cathedral. On this island there stands, in glorious isolation, the enclosed Poor Clare Convent, where the Poor Clare sisters have perpetual adoration of our Lord in the Blessed Sacrament, and observe the rules of penance and silence. They spend their lives there quite unaware that James Joyce immortalises Nun's Island in his greatest short story *The Dead*.

A main road divides Nun's Island in two. A continuous line of houses border the road. The houses have each a little garden which runs down to the river Corrib. A study of the area now reveals that it would be impossible to get into the back garden of any of the houses there except through the front door or by fording the rapids of the river Corrib, a feat which would be rather foolhardy.

If we accept that Michael Furey came to the back garden to serenade Gretta, as being factual, we are faced with many imponderables. For there is no trace or tidings of any Michael Furey dying anywhere in Co. Galway in the years 1900 to 1907 when *The Dead* was written. Again looking at the layout of Nun's Island now – and it has not changed very much – the feat of entering the back garden of any house there except through the front door of the house seems impossible. And one does not enter through the front door and then go out to serenade.

One puzzling fact remains. Where did James Joyce pick up the name Nun's Island. Of course Nora Barnacle told him. But why. I suggest that Nun's Island was the trysting place of Nora and Sonny Bodkin and later of Nora and Willie Mulvagh. Here, sheltered by the high walls that surrounded the former jail, Nora was safe to walk with her lovers, safe from the eyes of the gossipers and her uncle and guardian Thomas Healy.

The inclusion of Oughterard in the story of *The Dead* can

easily be explained. Oughterard is a beautiful name. It is pleasing to the ear and tongue. James Joyce had heard from Nora Barnacle that her father was working in Oughterard and may have concluded that the Barnacle paternal home was near there. Joyce, as yet, had never been to Galway and so had no clear idea of the geography of these places or their relation to one another. He only knew that Oughterard was in the west of Ireland, situated near Galway at the gate of Connemara. To a Dublin man such a place was in "far Connaught", and was a suitable place to bury honourably the first love of Gretta Conroy.

It is interesting to recall here that when James Joyce visited Galway in August, 1912 he wrote a long letter to his brother Stanislaus in Trieste under the date, August 7th. In this letter he writes "I cycled to Oughterard on Sunday and visited the graveyard of *The Dead*. It is exactly as I imagined it and one of the headstones was to J. Joyce." There is no question in this letter of saying or implying that Michael Bodkin or even a Michael Furey was buried in Oughterard. All he says in his letter to Stanislaus is that it was the graveyard of *The Dead*. He doesn't imply that he visited any grave there. If he had visited a particular grave then surely he would have mentioned it in this letter.

In the same year, 1912, Joyce visited Rahoon cemetery with Nora and soon wrote a poem in which he tried to express Nora's feelings and inner thoughts as she visited the tomb of her dead lover, Sonny Bodkin:-

She Weeps Over Rahoon
Rain on Rahoon falls softly, softly falling
Where my dark lover lies.
Sad is his voice that calls me, sadly calling
At grey moonrise.

Love, hear thou
How soft, how sad his voice is ever calling,
Ever unanswered and the dark rain falling,
Then as now.

34

Dark too our hearts, O love, shall lie and cold
As his sad heart has lain
Under the moongrey nettles, the black mould
And muttering rain.

The conclusion is crystal clear. (Michael) Sonny Bodkin lies buried in Rahoon. He had no connections whatever with Oughterard. Oughterard's claim to fame is based on its use in the story of *The Dead* which is an imaginative story into which Joyce has weaved many threads of fact and fiction.

Nora Barnacle had been very much in love with the youthful Michael — Sonny Bodkin. His death had a traumatic effect on the sixteen years old Nora. She withdrew from life for a while and pined to herself. But she was young and resilient and quite soon she returned to her former self. It seems that when she was broken-hearted at the death of Sonny Bodkin she confided in a priest. We have already noted how, when in 1904 she told James Joyce about her love affairs in Galway, she mentioned an incident between her and a curate in the city. She told Joyce about getting tea at the Presbytery, about their little chats and even about an indiscretion committed by the priest.

Strangely she didn't give the priest's name. There is a note in *Exiles* which reads "Bodkin died, Kearns died." This suggested to me that perhaps the priests name was Kearns. The records of the Galway Diocese reveal that there were two priests of the surname Kearns (Kerin, Kieran) ministering in the diocese in the period 1895-1904, but neither of them in that period or at any time, was a curate in the city of Galway. They both served all their priesthood lives far away from Galway city. Fr. Patrick Kerin (Kearns) was P.P. of Carron, in North Clare from 1891 to 1899 after which he was appointed P.P. of Ballyvaughan. Fr. Michael Kerins (Kearns) was Administrator of Peterswell 1895 - 1899 when he was appointed P.P. of Carron. Thus whoever the Kearns was whom Joyce mentions in his notes in *"Exiles"* he was not a Priest.

I have some difficulty in accepting Joyce's story that Nora had "tea at the presbytery." The presbytery adjacent to her home was in Market Street in the centre of the city. It was about fifty metres from her mother's home in Bowling Green and was familiar to countless generations of Galwegians under the title "College House." As Presbyteries go it was unique in that it housed two parish priests and four curates. It was a large three storied building. The parish priests lived on the first floor and the curates above them on the second floor. The kitchen and dining room were on the ground floor. A young handsome lady could not be entertained in College House with all the 'comings and goings' of priests in that house.

Any information regarding the priest's identity is vague and uncertain. There is a possibility that he may be the Fr. Moran described in Stephen Hero as attending Gaelic League meetings in Dublin around 1900. This Fr. Moran "had a neat head of curly black hair and expressive black eyes". He "was a pianist and sang sentimental songs and was for many reasons a great favourite with the ladies". The possible tie-in with Nora's story is that there was a curate, Fr. Moran, active in the west of Galway city about 1900. But there the similarity ends. The curate Fr. Moran was a tall blond headed man who lived in lodgings in Sea Road (then the western limit of the city) and so could not "have tea at the presbytery".

And yet Nora Barnacle did tell Joyce about her friendship with a curate. Joyce mentions this fact in two distinct letters. On December 3rd 1904 he mentioned it in the letter to his brother Stanislaus where he is telling him something about Nora's background. He mentions the episode again in a letter he wrote to Nora Barnacle on 19th August 1912 in which he says to her "They speak of my verses as 'exquisite and passionate poems.' Can your friend in the soda water factory or the priesteen write my verses". Here Joyce is in a jealous mood, comparing himself with Nora's previous lovers and he numbers "your friend in the soda factory" and "the priesteen" as his two great rivals.

"Your friend in the soda factory" refers to the last love affair Nora had in Galway. Mary O'Holleran Morris, in her account of Nora Barnacle as quoted by Richard Ellmann, tells us that some time after the death of Sonny Bodkin, Nora met Willie Mulvey.

> "She just met him on the bridge. He asked her would she meet him and Nora said to me 'Mary what will I do.' I told her to go with him".

This Willie Mulvey is the Protestant Joyce mentions in his letter to Stanislaus, 3rd December 1904. There was parental disapproval of the affair, the violent consequences of which forced Nora to leave Galway and seek out her life elsewhere

In Molly Bloom's famous soliloquy in *Ulysses*, Molly (Nora Barnacle) remembers Bloom's courtship of her and unlocks her innermost thoughts when he proposed to her "he asked me to say yes and I wouldn't answer first, only looked out over the sea and the sky I was thinking of so many things he didn't know of Mulvey and .... and how he kissed me under the Moorish wall."

Who was this Willie Mulvey. Many students of Joyce have failed to, or have been misled in their efforts, to identify him. The reason for the confusion stems, it seems, from the spelling of his name. If I were to ask any of the old people in Galway city if they knew a Willie Mulvey, the answer would be a definite no. But if you ask them did they know a Willie Mulvagh (pronounced Mulva) the answer is quite firm "I knew him well."

Willie's sister Henrietta Mulvagh lived in the family home in Mary Street until she was hospitalised in Merlin Park Galway in 1974. Henrietta (Hetty to her friends) died in June 1978. She was a charming person, full of humour and good sense. She was very clear in all her facts and very careful in giving the full picture of her brother Willie. She first established that her brother Willie had a love relationship with Nora Barnacle.

She was eight years old in 1904 and clearly remembered Nora Barnacle and the trauma her brother Willie went through when Nora left Galway. She described Nora for me as "a handsome, beautiful girl, with lovely auburn hair and Willie was deeply in love with her. She was a charming girl.

She was the daughter of very respectable and highly respected parents. Willie was very upset when Nora left Galway".

Hetty shared with me many facts about her family. Her father Robert Mulvagh was a sergeant in the R.I.C. (the Royal Irish Constabulary was the name given to the police force in Ireland from 1840 until the Garda Siochana was established in 1922). Robert Mulvagh was a native of Sligo, as was his wife Mary Thompson. Robert served in the R.I.C. in many stations in Co. Galway. He served in Barnaderg, Oranmore and finally Galway city.

There were nine children in the family of whom Willie was the eldest and Henrietta the youngest. Hetty was not sure where Willie was born. She thought he was born in Barnaderg, Co. Galway but a search in the county register of births did not establish this. Willie whose Christian names were William George received his national school education in the national schools in the towns where his father was stationed. The fact that he was a Protestant meant of course that he was free to absent himself from the Catechism or Religious Instruction class from 12.30 to 1 p.m. each day. Each day at 12.30 p.m. the teacher turned the public notice board from Secular Instructions to read Religious Instruction. Religious Instruction was always given during lunch hour, in order to satisfy the statute which declared National Schools as being non-denominational.

When Willie Mulvagh graduated from the national school, he attended the Grammar School in College Road, Galway and soon was apprenticed to the office of Joe Young's Mineral Water Co. in Eglington Street, Galway. He then availed of correspondence courses and, by dint of private studies, he qualified as an auditor and an accountant. His father was now transferred from Oranmore to Eglinton Street Barracks, Galway. The family found accommodation in Mary Street where they rented a house from Joe Young, a Mineral Water manufacturer. Here the family of Mulvagh lived from 1901 to the hospitilisation of Hetty in 1974.

Willie Mulvagh worked first as accountant in the firm of

Joe Young in Eglinton Street just around the corner from Mary Street, where the restaurant 'The Lion's Tower' now stands. James Joyce, in a letter to Nora Barnacle in 1912, wrote "Can your friend in the Soda Water factory .... write my verses." The reference is clearly to Willie Mulvagh and his work in Joe Young's mineral water factory.

After working in Joe Young's for a number of years Willie Mulvagh started a private practice as an accountant and auditor living in Montpelier Terrace. Here he married and reared his family. Here he remained until he retired. On retiral he joined his son Desmond in London where he died in 1952, at the age of 70.

In his book *James Joyce's Disunited Kingdom* John Garvin's account of the life of Willie Mulvagh is misinformed. The Mulvagh family never lived in Bohermore (a northern outskirt); their only city residence was in Mary Street, not much more than one hundred metres from Bowling Green. Nor is it true to say that Willie Mulvagh ever served in the British Army or visited Gibraltar. His brother Edward was the only one of the Mulvagh family to fight in the Great War. Edward married a girl from Galway and lived in Waterlane, a terrace off Bohermore.

Two of Willie Mulvagh's sisters were killed in accidents in Belfast. Florry (Florence) was matron of the hospital in Gibraltar where she married the chaplain, the Rev. Jim Johnston. Later, when they transferred to Belfast, Florry was knocked down by a motor-bike and killed. Her sister Frances married a head Constable of the R.I.C. named Parke, and she, poor creature was killed by a car as she stepped off a bus in Belfast.

By a strange quirk of fate William Mulvagh later figured as an important witness to the abduction and murder of Fr. Michael Griffin by the Auxiliaries on the night November 14th/15th 1920, in what must be regarded as one of the most dastardly acts in the Irish War of Independence. Fr. Griffin was 28 years of age and had been ordained just three years previously. He was a C.C. in Ennistymon 1917-1918 and was then transferred to St. Joseph's parish, in Galway city where he ministered until his death in 1920. Fr. Michael Griffin lived with his fellow curate Fr. O Meehan at 2, Montpelier Terrace, in Sea Road.

On the night of November 14th 1920 Fr. Griffin was lured from this house at about 11.40 p.m. and his body was recovered from a shallow grave, at Cloughnascoilte, near Barna village on Saturday 20th November 1920 with the marks of a bullet which had passed through his brain. This is not the occasion to probe the question why was Fr. Griffin shot. It is sufficient to say they were troubled times, and in such times men do not behave logically or reasonably. Fr. Griffin's support of the Republican movement was on the civil, economic and cultural side. At that time Willie Mulvagh lived at No. 3 Montpelier Terrace, next door to the house of the two priests Frs. O Meehan and Griffin.

On November 22nd 1920 at Eglinton Street police station three military officers opened an enquiry into the death of Fr. Griffin. They first went to St. Joseph's Church where they viewed the remains. They then returned to the barracks and proceeded to take evidence. Drs. Sandys and M. G. O'Malley gave evidence that the cause of death was a bullet which passed through the brain. It went in at the right temple and out at the left temple.

Then Mr. William Mulvagh came forward and gave evidence. He lived next door to Fr. Griffin at Montpelier Terrace. On the night of Sunday November 14th his attention was attracted by knocking at about 11.40 p.m. He was in bed at the time and he thought the knocking was at his own door. At first the knocking was like the sound of fists on the door. Then it became more intensified as if it was done with sharper instruments like the ends of revolvers. He looked out the window. The window was not opened. It was very stormy and he could only get a side view of the entrance to Fr. Griffin's. Mr. Mulvagh saw two men with their hats in their hands going up the steps to the door. The first man called to the second "come on" and then the two entered the house. The men were about five feet eight or nine and of medium build. They wore light coats. A third man who stayed on the footpath wore a belted coat. All wore ordinary soft trilby hats. When the men went in Fr. Griffin's door Mr. Mulvagh, presuming that it was an ordinary raid, retired to his bed and heard no more. A very interesting point about Mr. Mulvagh's evidence is that he judged from what he saw that the visit to Fr. Griffin's house was a 'police raid' rather than a pastoral visit to a priest. Most people presumed that Fr. Griffin on that fatal night was lured to his death on the pretence of being called out on a sick-call.

When, in 1904, Tommy Healy, Nora's uncle and guardian, discovered that she was walking out with a Protestant Willie Mulvagh, he was furious and left Nora under no delusions about his opinion of her conduct. Nora was forced to meet Willie in secret and with an alibi of attending devotions at the Abbey Church in Francis Street. One night her luck ran out, and she met her uncle as she walked with Willie. Her uncle exploded and ordered her home. He followed her step by step to their home in Whitehall. When he got her inside their home he exercised his 'parental' discipline over her. He lashed her with his tongue for quite a while and then in a fit of temper he struck her with his hand and walking stick and left her sore and sorry.

The relationship between Nora and her uncle had never been very warm or friendly but now it reached breaking point. Nora was positively afraid of her uncle. If she were to live an honourable independent life there was only one thing for her and that was to leave her uncle's house. To do this was to leave Galway. Otherwise she would be for-ever under the fear and influence of her uncle. Nor could her mother in Bowling Green help her in her dilemna because mother would take sides with her brother Tommy and equally condemn the bold conduct of her wayward daughter. So the die was cast.

Sometime in January or March 1904 Nora Barnacle absconded from Galway and soon stepped into the pages of literature and history. As the train that bore her to Dublin pulled out from Galway station she had no idea of what life had in store for her. She was then aged almost twenty years of age and was in the full bloom of womanhood.

Nora had grown up in a strong Catholic environment. She was a member of the League of the Cross Sodality, known to Galwegians as "the Angels", while she was at the national school. On leaving the national school, she became a member of the Sacred Heart Sodality. Membership of the Sodalities meant going to Confession once a month and to Holy Communion in the Pro-Cathedral on Sodality morning The Sodality was well regimented and the absence of a member from a Sodality meeting was noted and the priest chaplain duly informed.

Nora Barnacle was faithful to her Sodalities although her work as portress often meant that she missed a meeting. Her mother was a woman of deep devotion and often chided and advised and encouraged her children in spiritual matters. Nora's contact with the nuns must have impressed her and given her a healthy outlook on life.

Yet despite the solid foundation on which her faith was based, little by little the foundation was nibbled at until the weakness of the flesh almost destroyed it. The nuns may have offered their sincere advice to her on her departure from her job as portress. Her mother certainly appealed to her that whatever else she did she must always remain faithful to the Mass and her prayers. Nora assured them that she would and probably in her heart meant it, but the seeds of revolt had already been sown. The foundations of her faith were shaking if not tottering.

Nora was a pleasant, warm, handsome, simple and, in many ways, an innocent girl. She had of course tasted of many of the hardships of life and had often been rocked and buffeted by them. She had too been trained and hardened by the strict discipline of a puritanical uncle. Because of the circumstances of her departure Nora had a sour taste in her mouth. She felt she had been treated very unfairly by her uncle and the principles he stood for. After all she had to leave Galway because of her friendship with a Protestant boy. She felt that her Catholic faith and her

42

upbringing, which she could not understand and which would not tolerate such a friendship, was overbearing and too demanding and she was prepared to examine it critically and even with hostility. Further, she felt that her person and dignity had been insulted and belittled by no others than by her nearest and dearest, her own flesh and blood. So she carried with her from Galway grievances and grudges which were to colour her future life.

CHAPTER 3

EXILE

In Dublin, Nora found employment at Finn's Hotel at 1 and 2 Leinster Street off Nassau Street, as a chambermaid cum waitress. The hotel was a middle class establishment with the emphasis on big meals rather than comfort and conveniences. Here Nora was happy with her work, and because of her pleasant manner she endeared herself to all. Every second evening she was free from hotel work and often chose to ramble around the strange large city of Dublin, and see its wonders.

She was a tall, striking young woman with a beautiful head of auburn hair and many is the man who met her and turned his head in amorous pursuit. Some men were bold enough to proposition her, but she was equal to the demands and the propositions. Once a guest in the hotel, a Mr. Holohan, had approached her and in trying to win sexual favours from her produced a French Letter to assure her of his concern for her feelings but Nora rejected his advances. There were other suitors less bold than Mr. Holohan but these too she succeeded in keeping at bay.

On June 10th 1904, Nora walked down Nassau Street for her afternoon stroll. She was walking by the grounds of Trinity College with not a care in the world when James Joyce stood in front of her and spoke to her. When she recovered her composure she spoke to him. They exchanged pleasantries and in some mysterious way found they were mutually attractive to one another. Joyce was dressed rather bizarrely, sporting a sailor's cap, and canvas shoes. Nora, not very skilled in all the nuances of the Dublin accent, thought at first that he was a sailor from some far-off land, perhaps from Sweden.

She saw in him some of the features of her first love, Michael Bodkin, and so as she gazed into his sharp blue eyes, Nora was already coming under his influence. Their conversation progressed to the point where they agreed to meet again on June 14th which was the first free evening available to them. They agreed to the corner of Merrion Square as the trysting place; in front of Sir William Wilde's house. I wonder did Nora realise that Sir William's ancestors had a house in Mary Street, Galway quite near her own ancestral home.

Nora Barnacle failed to keep the appointment on June 14th to the great disappointment of Joyce who had already been boasting to his friends about his new-found love.

Joyce immediately wrote Nora a note appealing to her to meet him:-

"I may be blind. I looked for a long time at a head of reddish-brown hair and decided it was not yours. I went home quite dejected. I would like to make an appointment but it might not suit you. I hope you will be kind enough to make one with me − if you have not forgotten me !"

15th June, 1904   James A. Joyce

(Letters 11, Page 42)

Nora had not forgotten James and they made an appointment for the evening of June 16th. June 15th was rather a disturbing and upsetting day for Joyce. He was behind in his rent and was given notice to quit by his landlord, the McKernans. His friends James and Gretta Cousins came to his rescue and gave him the hospitality of their home. His thoughts were centred on a singing tour of England, which he had planned in outline and which he had hoped would give him an uplift in life and job satisfaction. He had not as yet realised that he had fallen in love. His stroll with Nora on the evening of June 16th changed his plans and his life.

They walked towards Ringsend down by the river Liffey where nine years previously Joyce, as a young teenager, had met the pervert who had shocked and frightened him and undermined his moral upbringing. Joyce and Nora were opposites in so many things that at first it would be hard to find any one strand of life which they might hold in common.

Joyce was already a writer and had set his heart on becoming a great one. He was even then resolved to write about his spiritual experiences. To his aunt, Josephine Murray he had confided "I want to be famous while I am alive." He was even then moving amongst the giants of Anglo-Irish writings, and he was welcome at the table of Yeats, A.E., Shaw, Lady Gregory, Gogarty, George Moore, Padraic Colum, Synge and others.

But Joyce had already broken with his Anglo-Irish friends and had become a European in the broadest sense. He was attracted by Nietzsche, Abbas, Sendwogins, Bruno and other authors, all of whom had revolted against the Establishment and Authority. He had already decided that he could only reach full stature by going into exile. His experiment, and it was going to be an experiment, in living his peculiar type of life required that he leave Ireland. He had not lived with his family since some days after his mother's death in August 1903. He felt no warmth for his brothers and sisters: They were nothing to him. He was as he said in the Holy Office "unfellowed, friendless and alone."

Nora Barnacle was not in any way interested in art or literature. She had never felt the urge to read anything other than to glance at the local newspaper or the current magazines. She would find it hard, and did find it hard, to read anything with a deeper meaning than what the words plainly meant. Indeed, to the very end of her days, she failed to understand most of what Joyce wrote and in many cases refused to read it.

But despite these deficiencies in literature and art Nora Barnacle had wonderful personal qualities as a woman. She had a rare combination of innocence and earthiness. True to her name she was faithful and constant as the barnacle on the sea rock. She was loyal and dependable and trustworthy She was kind and tender and had a good sense of humour.

Like Joyce Nora too had cut adrift from her family. Because of her fosterage with her grandmother she had no great feeling for her parents or sisters or brother. Her uncle

Tommy's physical reprimand of her had left her with very bitter feelings towards her family. So Nora too was "friend-less and alone." Nora Barnacle and James Joyce were very much birds of a feather.

As they strolled towards Ringsend they were very open with each other. Joyce questioned Nora in much detail about her family, her early life and friends in Galway, with particular attention to her boyfriends there and her romances. He was like an explorer discovering some new river. He wended his way step by step back to the source of her life and explored all the tributaries that formed the main stream of her life. On his side Joyce was open and honest with Nora and gave her in much detail the story of his family and life.

Joyce was beginning to fall in love with Nora. He was beginning to understand what love means "the desire of good for another" as he tells us in his notes for *Exiles*. Joyce must often have longed to experience pure love — and now when he met it he was thrilled to feel the first warmth of a new relationship where gradually soul was meeting soul.

They were both interested in each others sexuality as their later letters reveal. And soon they engaged in a little love play. In this Nora took a positive role and aroused Joyce without any prompting from him. Later he recalled that encounter at Ringsend as "a sacrament which left in me a final sense of sorrow" and again "the recollection of it fills me with amazed joy." The episode affected Joyce profoundly and he kept searching for an opportunity of arousing Nora. But Nora resisted all his advances and often spoke rather bluntly to him, showing character and moral fibre.

In a strange way their love matured over the summer of 1904. Again and again Nora had to listen to a detailed account of his sexual history; his encounters with prostitutes and perverts; a rather sordid story for innocent ears and a pure heart. Gradually he undermined her standards and principles by telling her that he rejected all that was hitherto near and dear to her - home, style of life, tenets of her faith and moral principles. Naturally, Nora was very upset with these attacks on her beliefs. The tragedy for her was that she stood in Dublin a lone Galway girl, without support, without a close friend into whose ear she might pour the doubts and questions that haunted her.

One quality above all others attracted her to Joyce - it was his absolute candour. He opened his soul to her in its entirety and never attempted to hide from her even his most secret thoughts. The woman and the mother in her appreciated this candour. It enabled her to understand this mysterious man, and in her efforts to comfort and console him she gradually found herself in love with him. Joyce assured her that he had great and deep respect for her love. Her soul was to him "the most beautiful and simple soul in the world.'

Joyce was very proud of his friendship with Nora. He spoke of her with warmth to his friends, who knowing him smiled and waited to hear of the end of the friendship. On hearing that Joyce had a girl friend, his closest friend Vincent Cosgrave, who had walked with, and talked intimately with Joyce when they were both students at U.C.D., and who may have visited brothels with him, now decided that he would meet and make advances to Nora.

Vincent Cosgrave told Nora in no uncertain manner that she should avoid Joyce for her own sake, as he was unstable and his love would not last. Vincent paid court to Nora but she would have none of him and rejected all his advances. When she told Joyce about the treachery of his friend Joyce looked on Nora's rejection of Cosgrave as proof that she was now firmly attached to him and it flattered him no end. The incident bound them more closely together.

All during July and August they wrote notes and letters to one another. In a letter to Nora on the 1st September 1904 Joyce writes "Please remember that I have thirteen letters of yours at present." Not at all a bad count for a pair who met practically every second night. Joyce's introd-

uctions to his letters to Nora progressed from a blank in
June to "my dear little goodie-brown-shoes" in early July
– then to my "particular pouting Nora" in late July until
finally he wrote "my dear Nora" at the very end of July
and later "sweetheart". At first he signed himself "James A.
Joyce", then "Anjey", then "Jim", then "J.A.J." until at
the end of August he is always "Jim". For Nora there were
none of these difficulties in introduction and signature. She
boldly addressed Joyce as "my dearest" and signed them
"Nora".

The reaction of Joyce's friends to his courtship of Nora
Barnacle was rather strange. Most of them looked askance
as the friendship developed. All posed the question "How
could a man of such talents and such promising genius
consort with an uneducated girl who had no understanding
of literature and cared less about it?" Perhaps part of the
answer is given by his brother Stanislaus who, a few years
previous, painted the following pen-picture of Joyce:-

"Jim is a genius of character. When I say 'genius' I say
just the least little bit in the world more than I believe;
yet remembering his youth and that I sleep with him, I
say it. Scientists have been called great scientists because
they have measured the distance of unseen stars and yet
scientists who have watched the movements in matter
scarcely perceptible to the mechanically aided senses
have been esteemed as great, as Jim is, perhaps, a genius
though his mind is minutely analytic. He has, above all,
a proud wilful vicious selfishness out of which by times
now he writes a poem or an epiphany, now commits the
meanness of whim and appetite, which was at first protestant egoism, and had perhaps, some desperateness in
it, but which is now well-rooted – or developed? in his
nature, a very Yggdrasil.

He has extraordinary moral courage... His great passion
is a fierce scorn of what he calls the 'rabblement' – a
tiger-like, insatiable hatred. He is a distinguished appearance and bearing and many graces: a musical singing and
especially speaking voice (a tenor), a good undeveloped

talent in music, and witty conversation. He has a distressing habit of saying quietly to those with whom he is familiar the most shocking things about himself and others, and moreover, of selecting the most shocking times for saying them not because they are shocking merely, but because they are true... His manner however is generally very engaging and courteous with strangers, but, though he dislikes greatly to be rude, I think there is little courtesy in his nature. Not that he is not gentle at times, for he can be kind and one is not surprised to find gentleness in him. (He is always simple and open with those that are so with him). But few people will love him, I think, in spite of his graces and his genius and whosoever exchanges kindness with him is likely to get the worst of the bargain."
(Joyce, Stanislaus, *My Brothers Keeper*
London: Faber, 1958, pp. 18-19)

When he discovered Joyce was in love, Stanislaus was to remark on Nora's pretty manner, but thought her a little common. He felt Joyce never handled any affair as badly.

To those who considered that Nora was beneath him, Joyce gave the perfect answer when he wrote to Nora "Certain people who know that we are much together insult me about you. I listen to them calmly, disdaining to answer them, but their least word tumbles my heart about like a bird in a storm."

Before Joyce met Nora Barnacle he had a drink problem, as had his father and brother Charles. Neither his character nor his habits changed when he developed his love relationship with Nora. He was in a drunken brawl in Stephen's Green on the very day that Nora was writing to him as "her precious darling." He was picked from the gutter outside the National Theatre in Camden Street on June 20th. It is a moot point whether he ever told Nora of this great weakness of his. It was something she had to learn to live with, and suffer with for the rest of their lives together.

Whatever about the drink problem, Nora was considerably attracted by Joyce. The attraction blinded her to his faults

50

and failings. Gradually the attraction grew into love. Every second night Nora was free from duty in the hotel and on these nights Joyce called for her and together they would stroll around College Green, St. Stephen's Green and Merrion Square.

Occasionally they would attend a drama or concert, while all the time they grew closer to one another. Nora was thrilled when on August 22nd she heard Joyce sing for the first time in public at an evening concert, where he sang 'The Coulin' and 'My love she was born in the North Countree'. Her joy overflowed when Joyce shared the platform with John McCormack and J. C. Doyle on the last night of the Dublin Horse Show in a concert in the Antient Concert Rooms. In deference to Nora he sang Yeat's beautiful lyric 'Down by the Sally Gardens' which speaks so tenderly of youth and love. A critic said of Joyce "Mr. Joyce possesses a light tenor voice which he is inclined to forces on the high notes but sings with artistic emotionalism".

Nora was so impressed and delighted with Joyce's performances at these concerts that she said later that 'Jim should have stuck to music instead of bothering with the writing". There is some evidence that Nora Barnacle had a sweet singing voice herself and that often as she strolled the Dublin streets with Joyce she swopped melodies and songs with him.

One song she sang for him impressed Joyce because of its story and theme and was found worthy to find a place in his great story *The Dead*. The "Lass of Aughrim" tells the story of a woman who had been seduced and then cast aside by her seducer Lord Gregory. In the song she comes to her lover's home with her baby begging admission and acceptance but coldly, very coldly he abandons her.

If you'll be the lass of Aughrim
As I am taking you mean to be
Tell me the first token
That passed between you and me.

51

Oh don't you remember
That night on you lean hill
When we both met together
Which I am sorry now to tell

The rain falls on my yellow locks
And the dew it wets my skin
My babe lies cold within my arms
Lord Gregory, let me in.

It was now obvious to Joyce that he was in love with Nora. He had the tenderest of feelings for her and was prepared to let his friends know this. They, who knew him as a student in U.C.D. and who understood his lifestyle, were astounded that he should show interest in a particular woman and in one who was so far his inferior intellectually.

But Joyce had a dilemma. To tell or not to tell the truth about himself and his lifestyle. He felt that in all honesty he should bare his soul to her and take the consequences. He felt that she should know the inner Joyce with its light and shade so that there would be no misgivings, no mis-understandings. There were two areas of his life which, however embarrassing, he felt she must know if she were to commit herself completely to him. Nora must know him with all his warts as he knew himself.

One night in August as they strolled around the Park, Joyce gave Nora a full picture of his sexual life before he met her. He told it in all its sordidness and Nora found it hard to accept it, though accept it she did. It was on that night that Nora revealed her love affairs in Galway. Whatever compunction either felt about each other was resolved on that night. It was because it was resolved Joyce could write on 29th August to Nora about the choice now before him.

"While I was repeating this to myself I knew that life was still waiting for me if I chose to enter it. It could not give me perhaps the intoxication it had once given but it was still there and now that I am wiser and more controllable it was safe. It

52

would ask no questions, expect nothing from me
but a few moments of my life, leaving the rest
free, and would promise me pleasure in return. I
thought of all this and without regret I rejected it.
It was useless for me; it could not give me what I
wanted."
                    (Letters 11,   p. 49)
Without regret he was turning his back on sexual orgies: he
was rejecting them — because of his newlyfound love for
Nora.

But there was another area of his life which he now felt
in that honest way of his he must tell Nora all about. It
was his whole attitude to the Catholic Church, the Christian
faith and the social order. Somehow his nerve and courage
failed him when it came to telling Nora face to face of his
stand on religion. He was afraid that the revelation of his
irreligion would upset Nora and that her love for him would
not survive the shock. After all, she was a Catholic, who
practised her religion with fervour if not with full
conviction. Joyce had to put her love to the supreme test.
She must accept him with all his warts or else they would
part and go their separate ways.

In the same letter of the 29th of August, Joyce explained
his religious attitudes and beliefs. He wrote:-
"Six years ago I left the Catholic Church, hating
it most fervently. I found it impossible for me to
remain in it on account of the impulses of my
nature. I made secret war upon it when I was a
student and declined to accept the positions it
offered me. By doing this I made myself a beggar
but I retained my pride. Now I make open war
upon it, by what I write and say and do."
                    (Letters, 11, p. 48)
What of Nora? Joyce's letter to her of the 29th August
1904 was long and rambling. It told her of his mother's
painful illness and death. It dealt with so many matters of
such a personal nature that it caused Nora to shrug her
shoulders and wonder what sort of a man James Joyce

really was who now wanted "more than her caresses".

Joyce wrote to Nora again on 1st September 1904 hoping to put her "in better spirits" as she disliked Mondays and he concluded by smothering her with terms of endearment "my dear simple-minded, excitable, deepvoiced, sleepy and impatient Nora, a hundred thousand kisses".

While his love for Nora matured Joyce set up home with Gogarty in the Martello Tower, Sandycove on the 9th September 1904. They were soon joined by Samuel Chenevix Trench who was passionately interested in the Anglo-Irish revival. They were a motley trio. Joyce wished to have a roof over his head and peace and quiet to write "his novel" Gogarty was a student in Trinity College, a poet famous for his outlandish wit and ambition. Trench was an Oxford graduate, who had become such an insufferable. Irish Irelander that he called himself Diarmuid Trench. There was permanent tension in the Tower, so much so that Stanislaus Joyce, thought Gogarty would have put Joyce out of the Tower straight away were it not that he was afraid "that if Jim made a name some day it would be remembered against him (Gogarty)".

There is an interesting tie-in between Gogarty's maternal grand-parents and Nora Barnacle. Gogarty's mother was an Oliver from Galway. Her father, John Oliver of Eyre Square, had a bakery in Mainguard Street — roughly where the Barna Garden florists are now. Tom Barnacle worked for a time in this bakery.

Joyce stayed in the Martello Tower less than two weeks, 9th September to 19th September. It was during his ten days here that he proposed to Nora that they leave Ireland together and share a "hazardous life". When he left the Tower he lived with his mothers people, the Murrays for a few days and then he returned home to his father. He convinced his father that if he were to make his name in the world he must quit Ireland and become a European. He wished to be a writer and he felt that Ireland inhibited him from writing freely and openly on the subjects of his choice.

He was worried about Nora Barnacle. He had no money, no prospects, nothing to offer her except his love. He was haunted with the question should he ask her to come with him. He confided in his friend J.F. Byrne what was troubling his mind. Byrne wrung from Joyce a clear admission that he loved Nora very deeply "that he could not feel the same about any other girl." Byrne gave his decision "Don't wait and don't hesitate, ask Nora and if she agrees to go with you, take her".

Joyce asked Nora would she be prepared to leave Ireland with him and turn her back on kith and kin. In Joyce's letters of 10th, 16th and 19th September 1904 we can read between the lines the great struggle that went on in both their minds, to clarify and try to understand the difficulties and the full import of their decision. Joyce asked Nora again and again "are you sure you are not under any misapprehension about me?" .... when she had answered this question again and again in the affirmative it allowed him to burst forth "the fact that you can choose to stand beside me in this way in my hazardous life fills me with great pride and joy".

The fact that Nora was only twenty years of age and that from her early days she had cut adrift from her family in Galway and had now 'exiled' herself in Dublin left her very much a lone 'orphan' in Dublin with no one to guard and guide her. Nora had no one to help her make up her mind when Joyce asked her to emigrate with him. The decision was hers and hers alone. In fairness to Joyce he returned again to ask Nora to reconsider her decision to 'elope' with him. On the 19th September, he wrote to her "my object, however, was to find out whether with me you would be deprived of comforts which you have been accustomed to at home" and again, in a letter of 26th September 1904, he wrote to her "I often wonder do you realise thoroughly what you are about to do? .... I often doubt if you do realise it".

Nora had made up her mind and she was determined to go with Joyce and only one thing could prevent her: if any of her own people in Galway, the Barnacles or the Healys heard of the proposed adventure and came to Dublin and took her home. She discussed this problem with Joyce and he was fully aware of all the implications of her leaving Ireland. Joyce assured Nora that he would stand by her if her people interfered. He wrote to her on the 11th September 1904 "I intended to tell you that if you receive the least hint of any act on the part of your people you must leave the Hotel at once and send a telegram to me to say where I can see you. Your people cannot of course prevent you from going if you wish, but they can make things unpleasant for you."

In the meantime, the full preparations for departure were made. Nora had applied for a job in London and had been accepted and Joyce wrote to the employers on her behalf stating that she was willing "to accept their offer". But Joyce was hoping to get a teaching job in Paris and, in his letter to Nora of the 29th September 1904, he prepares her for a trip to Paris.

Joyce had accepted a teaching post from the Berlitz School in London. In early October he received a telegram from them asking him to go to Zurich. The fare to Zurich was £3.15.0, which he had not. He set about borrowing it from his literary friends. Lady Gregory sent him £5. George Russell (AE) sent him £1. Francis Sheehy-Skeffington refused to contribute and wrote to him "you have my best wishes for your welfare and for that of your companion which is probably much more doubtful than your own". As a last resort to get the fares he sent his brother Stanislaus around amongst his friends to make up the amount.

The boat sailed at 9 o'clock on the night of the 9th October 1904, from the North Wall. Nora Barnacle went aboard the boat separately unknown to Joyce's father and many of his friends. Padraic Colum reflecting on Joyce's departure wrote "there is no doubt that Joyce looked forward to a return to Ireland with Nora, when he would be recognised and honoured" and there is no doubt that was the dearest wish in his heart expressed again and again to

56

Nora.

Joyce left Dublin in the highest of spirits. He was bidding goodbye to a life of poverty and misery; he was launching out into the sea of hope and his dearest friend was by his side to comfort and console him. Nora had avoided the Joyce party that had come to the North Wall to wish bon voyage to James. Unnoticed, she had slipped aboard intending to surface only when the ship weighed anchor. But she was spotted on deck by a family friend, Thomas Devin, who immediately suspected that here was an elopment and straightaway poured his suspicions into the ears of Joyce's father, John. In a moment of doubt and disbelief John enquired what was the name of the romantic lass. On hearing it was Barnacle, John wittily said "She'll never leave him". Thus they sailed into exile. Sadly, they were never to live in Ireland again.

All through the night of 8th-9th October, the ship chugged its way to Liverpool and from there they took the mail train to London. In London, Joyce called at the home of Arthur Symons, hoping to borrow some money. He caused Nora great misery by leaving her alone in a London Park for over two hours while he was visiting Symons. She was certain he had abandoned her and would not return. Symons was a friend of authors in London and Paris and would most certainly have helped the two run-aways but unfortunately he was not then at home. There was nothing for it now but to travel on to Paris which they reached on the night of the 9th October.

Joyce had lived in Paris for four months in 1903, and so knew the city somewhat. Now, he visited old friends and pupils there in the hope of borrowing some money Joyce's old pupil Douce was away on holidays in Spain, but Dr. Joseph Riviere was most generous and lent Joyce sixty francs to help him get to Zurich. Once again, Joyce had left Nora sitting on a park bench where she suffered the awful trauma of loneliness, stranded as she was in a country where she knew not one word of the language of the people. Nora bought a postcard while she waited and wrote a very vague note to her mother in Galway, which gave no indication of her elopment but at least was an assurance that she was alive and well and was "seeing the world".

On the night of the 10th October, tired and bedraggled, they travelled by train from Paris to Zurich where they arrived early on the morning of the 11th of October. Confident that they had left all their black days behind them and assured that Joyce had a job as teacher, they booked into a hotel appropriately named Hoffnung, which means Hope.

Immediately, Joyce went to call on the principal of the Berlitz school to announce his arrival. He was dumbfounded to find that Miss Gilford had not been in touch with the principal Herr Malacrida and that there was no vacancy in the school. Crestfallen he returned to Nora to the Hotel Hoffnung. They were desperate. They were alone and they consoled one another as best they could all day, and that night slept together for the first time and consummated their love. They were in dire financial straits, penniless, jobless, almost hopeless. Joyce drew on his extraordinary gift of being able to borrow money from complete strangers and managed to survive for a whole week in Zurich.

During this week which Nora considered an eternity the two lovebirds could stand back and look at their position in relation to their families and in relation to one another. Nora felt ill at ease about her own family. In the eyes of the law she was a minor and so could be claimed by her family in Galway, if she could be traced through London, Paris and now Zurich. So she was very anxious to hear from Finn's Hotel, whether her people knew of her whereabouts and what was their reaction to her flight.

To add to this anxiety was the new one of her strange alliance with Joyce. It had not the firm assuring base of marriage either in a civil or religious ceremony and so in Nora's eyes there was always the nagging feeling that their elopement was but a fanciful trial-marriage and that some day she would find Joyce had flown from her side.

Joyce did his best to allay Nora's anxieties. He assured her that he pledged himself to her for life and that a religious or civil ceremony could not add anything to his personal pledge.

In all his letters to Dublin at the time he was always careful to ask Stanislaus whether the Barnacles in Galway were looking for the "missing" Nora. "Has she been advertised for in the papers in Dublin? She is however interested to know what went on in the Hotel (Finn's)." Meanwhile in all the turmoil and disappointment Joyce continued to write a new chapter of *Stephen Hero.*

After a week in Zurich living on their wits Herr Malacrida heard that there was a teaching job in Trieste and he sent Joyce and Nora to explore the possibility. They arrived in Trieste on the 20th October 1904. It was then the principal port of the Austrian Empire. Within an hour of arrival there Joyce through a misunderstanding was arrested and it took all the good graces of the British consul in Trieste to have him released. Meanwhile, Nora had to walk the streets abandoned and forlorn.

On release Joyce hastened to the Berlitz school to enquire about a vacancy. The vice principal of the school, Bertelli, regretted that there was no vacancy in the school. There was nothing for it but to search for another job. Joyce spent many days looking for private pupils tramping the streets of Trieste. He even sought unsuccessfully a job as English correspondent in a commercial company, and again had to fall back on borrowing 'right left and centre'.

At this juncture the principal of the Berlitz school came to Joyce's rescue. Almidano Artifoni offered Joyce a post as teacher 150 miles South of Trieste in a place called Pola. Pola was an international port like Trieste. Here was situated the dockyard and naval arsenal. The town was thronged with naval officers and soldiers.

Artifoni explained to Joyce that unmarried men were preferable as teachers. Joyce, despite his assurances to Nora, announced that he was not married but was travelling with a young woman. Artifoni couldn't get the logic of the answer and advised Joyce to sign all the papers as man and wife.

It is possible that on this advice Joyce and Nora had a

civil marriage in Pola around this time. In a letter to Stanislaus on 18th July 1931, he wrote "having eloped with my
present wife in 1904 she with my full connivance gave the
name of Miss Gretta Greene which was quite good enough
for il Cav. Fabbri who married us and the last gentleman in
Europe il conte Dandino who issued the legitimate certif-
icates for the offspring, but this full connivance voided the
marriage in the eyes of English law".

Joyce and Nora arrived in Pola on the 31st October 1904,
tired and ragged from travel. They immediately took a
dislike to the city. Nora found it a "queer old place" and
Joyce said of it "a back-of-God-speed place". Straightaway
they resolved to get away from Pola as quickly as possible.
Nora began to press Joyce to finish his great book so that
they could get away from that "boring place", "with its
hundred races and thousand languages" and its "multitude
of mosquitoes".

In the meantime Joyce and Nora moved into a furnished
room and kitchen in 2 Via Guilia just around the corner
from the Berlitz school. Joyce contracted to teach English
to naval officers for sixteen hours a week at a salary of £2
per week. The salary enabled them just to live. Joyce had
one suit of clothes and Nora had one dress which they never
changed. They had no fire and no stove and the weather
was now rather chilly. In a strange way they were happy
there and made some genuine friends and even entertained
them in their bed-sitter.

In the letter already quoted of the 3rd December 1904 to
his brother Stanislaus, Joyce gives an account of their
way of living which in many ways gives a full picture not
only of their struggle for existence but also of the growth of
their friendship and respect for one another. "as for our
way of living. We get out of bed at nine and Nora makes
chocolate. At midday we have lunch which we (or rather
she) buys, cooks (soup, meat, potatoes and something else)
in a locanda opposite. At four o'clock we have chocolate
and at eight o'clock dinner which Nora cooks. Then we go
to the Caffe Miramar where we read the Figaro of Paris and

we come back about mid-night."

Nora found it hard to settle in Pola. There was nothing for her to do. She had language problems and was not prepared to study any other language except French, looking forward to the day when they would settle in Paris. She had no interest in the writings of Joyce. In fact when Joyce read Chapter X1 for her she thought it "remarkable" "but she cares nothing for my art."

Nora was now beginning to influence Joyce's behaviour especially his drinking. Joyce wrote in December 1904, "my new relation (Nora) has made me a somewhat grave person and I have got out of the way of dissertations. I drink little or nothing, smoke vastly, sing rarely. I have become very excitable. Nora says I have a saint's face. Myself I think I have the face of a debauchee. But I am no longer so − at least I think I am not". Their friendship was deepening and they were able to forgive and forget their little quarrels. "Nora says they were lover's quarrels and says I am very childish. She says I have a beautiful character. She calls me simple-minded Jim".

Joyce was madly in love with Nora. It was the union of opposites. He was fragile, highly-strung, intellectual and witty and, in a sense, simple. She was robust, matter of fact, self-assured, practical with an apt turn of phrase. Joyce tried to mould Nora to his way of thinking but Nora would have none of it and through her life she retained her confidence in herself and her judgement which she was never ashamed to express. One night as they dined at the Caffe Miramar Nora expressed disapproval of Joyce's conduct by going silent and refusing to look at him. In desperation Joyce slipped her a note in which he threatened "to run up and down the cafe" if she did not look at him as she used.

By the 3rd December 1904, Joyce was fairly certain that Nora was pregnant and so he asked his brother Stanislaus to send him a medical account of conception and its effects on the mother. In a letter of the 28th December he wrote "Nora has conceived, I think". Joyce decided at this juncture to lean on Josephine, the wife of his maternal Uncle William Murray, to help Nora through her pregnancy. "She is away from all women except a little Fraulein and is of course adorably stupid on these points. You might write some kind of a generalising "don't be alarmed, my dear" letter as my own steely cheerfulness ..... is in need of some feminine supplement". He took the occasion in this letter which he wrote on the 31st December 1904, to pay Nora this glowing tribute "I have not been able to discover any falsehood in this nature (Nora) which had the courage to trust me".

Nora wrote to Aunt Josephine Murray asking for advice and help in her pregnancy. She could no longer bear the cold in the unheated room, which was their home, so she pressed Joyce to search for alternative lodgings. Joyce by now was very friendly with the principal of the school, Alessandro Francini, who offered them accommodation in his own house with the luxury of a stove and a writing desk. The Joyces moved into their new rooms by 13th January 1905.

About this time Stanislaus, Joyce's favourite brother, took issue with Joyce about Joyce's whole relationship with Nora. The row was prompted by a request by Joyce "to write to Signora Joyce" thereby implying that Nora had the status of wife. This annoyed Stanislaus and he told Joyce so, without mincing words. Joyce would not accept Stanislaus's criticisms of Nora and he was very fortright in his defence of her and of his own rights in a letter of 7th February 1905

"You are harsh with Nora because she has an untrained mind. She is learning French at present – very slowly. Her disposition, as I see it, is much nobler than my own; her love also is greater than mine for her. I admire her and I love her and I trust her – I cannot tell how much. I trust her. So enough."

(Letters, 11 79-80)

Further on in the same letter he wrote "I find your letters

62

dull only when you write about Nora." "So enough" gave Stanislaus the 'keep-off' sign in regard to Nora and left him under no illusions as to their deep relationship.

The Joyces settled down to a peaceful family life in Pola. They had musical evenings in their home. They bought new clothes and were just beginning to step out into society in Pola when suddenly the Austrian Government, having discovered a spy ring in Pola, decided to expel all foreigners from the city. Joyce was offered a teaching post in Trieste in the Berlitz school and was glad to leave Pola, "a naval Siberia".

It was early March 1905 when the Joyces arrived in Trieste. It was a seaport of considerable trade, of large squares and wide streets. It cared enough for the arts to have a theatre and opera house which were well patronised. It was a city in which East met West. Greeks, Albanians and Turks rubbed shoulders with Italians, French, and Germans.

The Joyces found lodgings at Piazza Ponterosso. It is sad to relate that when Nora's pregnancy became noticable the landlady asked her to find another flat. Early in April they moved to a more considerate landlady in the Via San Nicolo.

Soon a crisis developed in their married lives. It was caused by the combination of two factors. Joyce was drinking again and Nora was failing to cope with her pregnancy. It may have been true that Nora's unhappiness led to Joyce's drinking but it does not excuse his extreme behaviour even to the extent of being picked up out of the gutter.

Poor Nora had appealed for help and advice on maternity matters to Aunt Josephine Murray around the beginning of 1905 but so far she hadn't got an answer and she had no one in Trieste on whom she could lean because she was completely ignorant of the Triestino language. The result was she misinterpreted her symptoms and presumed that it was the great heat that made her weak, fretful and listless. She was very conscious too that whenever she walked the streets she was an object of scorn to the passers-by who commented on the poverty and unshapeliness of her dress and body. She suffered from morning illness and often sank into fits of crying and great silences. To add to her troubles she was sharing the kitchen with the landlady and she found that an impossible situation.

In such pitiful circumstances Joyce found consolation and relief in drink. This helped him too to sidestep Stanislaus who appealed to him to validate his union with Nora by either a civil or Church marriage. "But why should I have brought Nora to a priest or lawyer to make her swear away her life to me?" was his blunt answer.

Joyce was convinced that his calling in life was to be a great writer and became dissatisfied and impatient with teaching, "this seems to me on mature reflection a bloody awful position for me to be in. Some day I shall clout my pupils about the head, I fear and stalk out." The difficulties mounted. They were going through a great crisis and in July Joyce described at length his despair and dilemma in a long letter to Stanislaus.

"I must tell you some more things about Nora, I am afraid she is not of a very robust constitution. In fact she is not in good health. But more than this I am afraid she is one of those plants which cannot be safely transplanted. She is continually crying. I do not believe that she wants to have anything more to say to her people but I am quite sure (it is her own statement) that she cannot live this life with me much longer. She has nobody to talk to but me and, heroics left aside, this is not good for a woman. Sometimes when we are out together (with the other English 'professor') she does not speak a word during the whole evening. She seems to me to be in danger of falling into a melancholy mood which would certainly injure her health very much. I do not know what strange morose creature she will bring forth after all her tears and I am even beginning to reconsider the appositness of the names I had chosen ('George'

64

and 'Lucy'). She is also sensitive and once in Pola I had to turn the English teacher, a thoughless young chap named Eyers, out of the room (much as I dislike such an office) for making her cry. I asked her today would she like to rear a child for me and she said very convincingly that she would, but, in my present uncertain position I would not like to encumber her with a family. Her knowledge of even small affairs is very small and she cries because she cannot make the clothes for the child even after Aunt Josephine has sent her the patterns and I have brought the stuff for her...

I think it is best to be happy and honestly I can see no prospect of her being happy if she continues to live this life here. You know, of course, the high esteem I have for her and you know how quietly she gave our friends the lie on the night when she came with us to the North Wall. I think that her health and happiness would be much improved if she were to live a life more suited to her temperament and I don't think it right that even I should complain if the untoward phenomenon of 'love' should cause disturbance, even in so egoistically regulated a life as mine. The child is an unforgettable part of the problem. I suppose you know that Nora is incapable of any of the deceits which pass for current morality and the fact she is unhappy here is explained when you consider that she is really very helpless and unable to cope with any kind of difficulties.........

I have certainly submitted myself more to her than I have ever done to anybody and I do not believe I would have begun this letter but that she encouraged me. Her effect on me has so far been to destroy (or rather to weaken) a great part of my natural cheerfulness and irresponsibility but I don't think this effect would be lasting in other circumstances. With one entire side of my nature she has no sympathy and will never have any and yet once, when we were both passing through an evening of horrible melancholy, she quoted (or rather misquoted) a poem of mine which begins 'O, sweet heart, hear you your lover's tale'. That made me think for the first time in nine months that I was a genuine poet. Sometimes she is very happy and cheerful and I, who grow less and less romantic, do not desire any such ending for our love-affair as a douche in the Serpentine. At the same time I want to avoid as far as is humanly possible any such apparition in our lives as that abominable spectre which Aunt Josephine calls 'mutual tolerance'. In fact now that I am well on in my letter I feel full of hope again and, it seems to me, that if we can both allow for each other's temperaments, we may live happily. But this present absurd life is no longer possible for either of us."

(Letters, 11, 94-95)

Ever since they arrived in Trieste in March, Joyce was very conscious of a certain incompatability between them as was Nora and to their credit they were prepared to talk about it and try to solve it. At first they thought their problem was a money one only and they resolved to over-come that in various ways. Nora suggested that her grand-mother, Catherine Healy, Whitehall, Galway, who died early in March 1897 must surely have left her money in her will and that they should claim it. Joyce wrote to Stanislaus asking him to investigate the case. Stanislaus discovered that Catherine Healy died intestate.

Joyce next looked for an agency for Foxford Tweeds in Trieste as a source of extra income; but this effort failed more because of liason difficulties between Trieste and Foxford than because of any lack of enthusiasm on Joyce's part. Thus their efforts to overcome the poverty and penury of their situation had failed. Not but that Joyce was earning a reasonable salary as a teacher. Their mode of living; dining out everyday constant borrowing and spending ensured that they were living beyond their salary. The Principal of the school read the situation well and refused to pay Joyce his salary in advance.

In desperation Joyce suggested to his brother Stanislaus that the solution of his problem was that by saving more of his meagre salary and getting Stanislaus to chip in "and with the two (salaries) we might take a small cottage outside Dublin in the suburbs, furnish it......as an experiment which need not continue longer than six months". "It is possible that my idea is really a terrible one .... but after nine months of my present life I am unable to see things with my former precision.......my present life........will end shortly: and that will be a great relief to everybody concerned".

The Joyces were plumbing the depths. Stanisalus in his answer from Dublin underlined the difficulties of the "small cottage in Dublin" idea and was not enamoured of it. The scheme was forgotten when on the 27th July, Nora gave birth to a bouncing boy. Joyce immediately sent a telegram to his brother, Stanislaus in Dublin reading "Son born, Jim". Aunt Josephine who had helped Nora over her difficult pregnancy was quoted as saying "Brave Nora" when Stanislaus brought her the happy news.

As Nora had no communication with her people in Galway ever since leaving Dublin in the previous October, it was not deemed proper to break the news there. So the Barnacle family were completely unaware of where Nora was: they knew nothing of her elopement and, in accordance with the old adage 'what they don't know won't trouble them', the Joyces decided to leave very well alone and not send any notice of the child's birth to the Barnacles in Galway.

Contrary to normal procedure in naming a new born baby where the mother takes the initiative and generally gets her way, in the case of the Joyces, James Joyce decided on the baby's name. Before the birth he had decided if the baby were a boy its name should be Giorgio. Yet when the baby

67

was already two months old in a letter to his brother on the 18th September 1905, he wrote "the child has got no name yet though he will be two months old on Thursday next. ....I think a child should be allowed to take his father's or mother's name at will on coming of age. Paternity is a legal fiction".

Despite this shilly-shallying the day soon came when the child was named Giorgio. The naming had to be of a private nature as there was no public registration of the birth. Joyce was struggling 'against conventions' and he could see no reason or purpose in having Giorgio baptised. He expressed his feeling very clearly when he wrote to his brother in May 1905, before the birth of Giorgio; "Why whould I super-impose on my child the very troublesome burden of belief which my father and mother superimposed on me."

There is no telling now of what arguments were engaged in between Nora and Joyce on the question of baptism. But once Nora had accepted that there was no need of going "to a priest or a lawyer to make her swear away her life in marriage", it would be quite easy to convince her that baptism could wait until Giorgio made the decision for himself. Meanwhile, Nora breast-fed her baby. Giorgio was a quiet baby. "He is very fat and very quiet. I don't know who he's like" Joyce wrote and added "he has the 'companions' (Nora's) eyes". "He is damnably fat and long and healthy".

On 25th September 1905, Joyce wrote a cry from the heart to his brother, Stanislaus that he must come to Trieste where there was a vacancy for an English teacher in the Berlitz school. Joyce was not so much interested in the welfare of his brother as he was in having for himself a crutch on which to lean. He was not prepared to settle down and take on the responsibilities of a wife and family. He drowned his sorrows once again in bouts of drinking. Nora, meantime, had to try to make do on halfpennies and then had to suffer the indignities of being told she could not manage a household. She at least stayed at home with the baby while Joyce, in that irresponsible flamboyant way of his, ate out in cafes, and consumed large quantities of wine in the toughest bars in Trieste.

Stanislaus was not yet twenty-one but the prospects in Trieste teaching English were more enticing than the clerkship of fifteen shillings a week in Dublin, and he was willing to take the plunge. Thankfully for Nora, Stanislaus arrived in Trieste towards the end of October 1905. Joyce's drinking was a constant source of tension between Nora and Joyce and it was a great relief when Stanislaus, who was a non-drinker, was prepared to drag Joyce home from the bistros of Trieste.

Stanislaus now lived with the Joyces but in a very unhappy relationship with his brother. Nora thought very seriously about going back to her family in Galway and while she did in fact write letters to tell them of her intentions she never actually posted them. Joyce, aware that Ibsen when he was dying in Christiania abandoned his wife, was now very keen on following his example. He even wrote to Aunt Josephine Murray that he was planning to leave Nora. His principal reason was because "Nora does not seem to make much difference between me and the rest of the men she has known and I can hardly believe that she is justified in this.....I am a little weary of making allowances for people."

Stanislaus helped the Joyces over this crisis by his advice, by appealing to Aunt Josephine in Dublin whose word was acceptable to both and by drawing on himself the anger of his brother. Whenever Joyce escaped from Stanislaus to have a bout of drinking Stanislaus ferretted him out and made him come home. When he had him home he wasn't beyond giving him a good hiding as well as a lashing of the tongue. Gradually Joyce began to control his drinking and the relationship between Joyce and Nora improved.

In February 1906, the Joyces moved home into a house with the Francinis in the suburbs of Trieste. Here they were fairly happy and in class Joyce was able to joke about Nora. "My wife is no good at anything except producing babies and blowing bubbles. If I'm not careful she'll follow up George the First by unloading a second male successor for the dynasty. No, No, Nora this game doesn't suit me''.

Gradually, Joyce was learning that Nora was an individual with a mind of her own and that in no way was she to be looked on as anyone's playmate. She was the heart of the family and the home and Joyce appreciated what all this meant. He had to admit that her qualities of loyalty, steadfastness and forebearance far outweighed the faults he found in her.

Joyce was now forced to make another change. The Berlitz school had run into financial difficulties and there was a grave danger that either Joyce or his brother Stanislaus or both would lose their jobs. Joyce had also run into censorship difficulties with the book *Dubliners* and was in a fit of pique with everyone. He was very happy to accept a post as a correspondence clerk in a bank in Rome. Once again Joyce and Nora, and now baby Giorgio, with their few belongings set out for new horizons. The Roman job carried with it the princely salary of £12.50 a month and there were also the prospects of having pupils learning English in the evenings after work. The future was rosy.

The Joyces travelled by train to Fiume: from there they took the night ferry to Ancona and thence by train to Rome. They arrived in Rome on 31st July 1906, and found lodgings in the Via Frattina. Rome's climate agreed with the Joyces. Their appetites improved and the family were all eating well. This imposed a strain on their resources and once again they had to appeal to Stanislaus in Trieste for financial help.

They were not however at all impressed by Imperial Rome. The Tiber frightened them. They were not used to such a large wide river. A week after his arrival in Rome he wrote to Stanislaus on 7th August 1906 that the whole district around the Colosseum was "like an old cemetery with broken columns of temples and slabs". The famous dome of St. Peter's fell far short of the beautiful dome at St. Paul's in London. He thought ancient Rome was very like the Coombe district in Dublin. "Rome reminds me of a

70

man who lives by exhibiting to travellers his grandmother's corpse". Another and a grave fault Joyce found with Rome "it had not one decent cafe".

The additional salary received for his work made no difference to Joyce's solvency. He was still drinking heavily and the move to Rome only meant that he had more money to spend on wine. True Joyce worked from dawn to dusk. He began work at 8.30 a.m. in the morning and apart from a mid-day break of two hours he worked on to 7.30 p.m. in the evening.

During the day, Nora would do the house chores and in the afternoon go to a cinema show with Giorgio. Then when Joyce got home they went out for dinner. The usual dinner was rather substantial, consisting of two slices of roast beef, two polpetti, a tomato stuffed with rice, part of a salad and a bottle of wine. They bought the meat cooked and took it to a wine shop where they were supplied with plates and cutlery.

At home Joyce and Nora slept in separate beds. They were planning their family as Joyce found the burden of rearing his first-born too much for his liking. They were managing fairly well until the landlady announced she was raising the rent in November. It was clear that she was annoyed with the drunken behaviour of Joyce as well as with the screaming and antics of Giorgio. When the Joyces did not leave voluntarily the landlady evicted them on 3rd December 1906. It was night when the eviction took place and it was raining heavily. They luckily found a temporary home in a hotel. For the next four days Joyce searched for a flat.

On the 8th December, they moved to two small rooms in the Via Monte Brianzo. Now they had only one bed, so they slept "lying opposed in opposite directions" the head of one towards the tail of the other ! The eviction and consequent stay in the hotel was very costly and it left the Joyces with a very poor opinion of Rome and Italy and their concern about human misery. When Giorgio was accidently struck by a cab-driver, who was wielding his whip carelessly,

Nora and Joyce got more annoyed with the Italians: "I am damnably sick of Italy, Italian and Italians" he wrote to his brother.

Joyce blamed Rome for the fact that he had no time while there to write and when Nora told him that despite their family planning   efforts she was pregnant again the Joyces decided that they had had enough of Rome and Italy.

In Rome the Joyces had made no friends, had found nothing to anchor them. Indeed the opposite was the reality: because of their poverty and penury they felt that they would be happier anywhere else in the world. The hours in the bank were long and because Joyce had to write more than two hundred letters a day he had no time to devote to writing and literature.

During his sojourn in Rome he wrote almost nothing. Painting and sculpture, studios and art galleries never impressed them and never stirred in them a feeling of seeing in them the perfection of one side of man's achievements. Even the choir in St. Peter's gave them only a little thrill and the Masses and liturgies they attended sometimes as diversions, never seemed to rouse them to any ecstasy.

In February 1907, the Joyces had had enough of Rome and Italy. Joyce resigned his job and only then thought of seeking another job away from Rome.Marseilles, because it was an international port, appealed to him, but in the short time available to him he failed to find a job there. There was nothing for them but to return to Trieste where Artifoni had kept his original job open for him.

The three arrived back in Trieste, after seven months in Rome on the 7th March 1907, tired and penniless. They returned to the home of Francini to whom they owed rent since 1906. After a few days with the Francinis they found rooms at the Via Santa Caterina. Joyce resumed his job as a teacher in the Berlitz school, though not on as good terms as those he left when he resigned the previous year. He began a new venture by writing three articles on the colonial relations between England and Ireland

and gave three lectures on Ireland at the University.

By July, Joyce was totally fed up with life and his teaching job and decided to apply for a job to the South African Colonisation Society. Before he could receive a reply he became sick with rheumatic fever and was removed to hospital. His recovery was very slow. Meanwhile, Nora's pregnancy reached the fullness of time and she gave birth to a baby girl, named Lucia Anna on 26th July 1907. It was of some significance that the delivery took place in the paupers ward as Nora's had in 1884. With both parents hospitalised brother Stanislaus looked after their rooms and the now demanding Giorgio. Indeed, at this time the real breadwinner for the Joyces was Stanislaus.

Joyce's illness dragged on through August and to add to his difficulties he resigned his job in the Berlitz school and put all his faith in getting private pupils. When Nora came home from hospital she was testy and demanding and dissatisfied with her rooms. Her life was in turmoil. Her husband in hospital; herself weak and sickly; Giorgio rushing around the room all day; Lucia Anna colicky, a real crybaby, a demanding child; Stanislaus glum and surly. Apart from the twenty crowns which the hospital authorities gave Nora in charity on leaving hospital she was totally dependant on the generosity of Stanislaus and he was neither friendly nor generous.

Joyce's illness gave him time to reflect and look at his life. Showing some strength of character he renewed his faith in himself and strengthened his resolve to become a world famous writer on his discharge from hospital He returned to writing and soon finished his most famous short story, *The Dead* . It is a story as we have already noted woven out of his own experiences of life as well as of experiences he learned from Nora.

On the 8th September 1907, Joyce told his brother Stanislaus that as soon as he had finished *The Dead* he would re-write 'Stephen Hero': he was also tossing around in his mind his great novel *Ulysses* which he hoped would develop into a book instead of a short story. But soon his eyes began to give him much trouble. He was drinking heavily again, so heavily that Stanislaus frequently picked him up from the gutters and often pummelled him in an attempt to cure his drink problem. Nora for her part tried to exercise moral pressure on him by threatening to have"the children baptised tomorrow" unless he gave up the drink; a threat which always brought Joyce to his senses.

About this time, Joyce wrote one of his few political articles "Ireland at the Bar". It was published in the local Triestine newspaper *Il Piccolo della Sera* on the 16th September 1907. Its central theme was the great injustices perpetrated on Ireland by England and the misrepresentation of the Irish by English journalists and politicans. To illustrate his article, Joyce refers to the Maamtrasna Murder trials, and more especially, that of Myles Joyce during November 1882.

The Maamtrasna Murders were a cause celebre in Galway, and would have been discussed around many a fireside during Nora's youth. Maamtrasna is on the shores of Lough Mask, North-West of Cong, about 35 miles from Galway. On the 2nd of February 1882, the local people seized the unpopular bailiffs of Lord Ardilaun, murdered them and, after tying them up in bags, threw their bodies into Lough Mask. Evidently, a John Joyce could identify the murderers, and there was a possibility that he might turn King's evidence.

Early on the morning of the 18th of August 1882, a group of hooded men came to warn John Joyce that if he gave evidence against them, his life would be forfeit. John Joyce recognized one or more of the raiders, and it is thought he named them for his family to hear. The raiders panicked and killed John Joyce, his wife, and mother, and three of his four children.

On the 22nd of August, fifteen local people were arrested, and charged with the murders. Early in September, nine of these were put on trial in Galway but, because there was a danger that a Galway jury might be prejudiced, the case was removed to Dublin.

Three of the accused, Patrick Joyce, Patrick Casey, and Myles Joyce, were tried separately and were sentenced to death by Judge Barry. Five others were jointly tried and were convicted, but were afterwards reprieved. On the 24th of November the condemned prisoners arrived back in Galway and, on the 15th of December, they were executed by hanging in Galway jail.

Galway city was greatly disturbed by these hangings. Soon a warden was spreading the story that the ghost of Myles Joyce was seen in the prison. Then word came out of the prison that whereas Patrick Joyce and Patrick Casey admitted they were guilty, they were both adamant that Myles Joyce had no part in the murders. Myles himself was reported to have said again and again "Táim cho saor leis an leanbh atá san gciabhán " (I am as innocent as the child in the cradle).

It later came to light that the prosecution had interfered with one of the witnesses, and that his evidence would have freed Myles Joyce. His innocence was vouched for in Partry Church near Ballinarobe on the 12th of August 1884 by Thomas Casey, the chief state witness, who himself had been arrested for the murder, but who had turned King's evidence. During a mission in the Church, Casey, with a lighted candle in his hand, admitted publicly, and in the presence of the Archbishop of Tuam, Dr. McEvilly, that he had given false evidence at the trial of Myles Joyce.

The Archbishop called for a public enquiry. The English Government sent two officials to Cong to conduct the enquiry. They discovered that not only had Casey gone back on his evidence, but that another state witness, one McPhilbin, was on the point of reneging. The state officials called the two witnesses before them and threatened to withdraw their state subvention unless they stood by their first evidence. The threat had the desired effect. Casey and McPhilbin duly signed a statement in the R.I.C. barracks in Partry that the public repudiation and disavowal of their court evidence was done in a attempt to win back the favour and respect of their neighbours.

Thus the enquiry ended. When Lord Spencer, Viceroy of Ireland, gave the result of the enquiry in the House of

Commons, the Irish Members under Parnell refused to accept it as a fair enquiry and, after four days debate, they almost toppled the Liberal Government.

The Maamtrasna Murders and the subsequent trials became one of more common popular tales in Ireland during the last decade of the nineteenth century, not only as sordid and terrible murders, but also as a classic example of British misrule and injustice in Ireland.

Nora Barnacle would have been familiar with the story, especially the trials and executions. Joyce would have drawn on her memory of it when writing his article. Indeed, the emphasis in the article is on the trial and execution of Myles Joyce and not on the enquiry.

Joyce describes how Myles Joyce and the other accused could not speak English, and the court had to resort to an interpreter. The result was a tragi-comedy, in which the accused's voluble answers were translated by one or two words. His guilt was declared proven, and he was condemned. Not even his executioner, Joyce continues, could make him understand him, and he kicked at the poor man's head to shove it into the noose. Myles Joyce ("the patriarch of a miserable tribe") became for Joyce the symbol of the Irish Nation at the bar of public opinion.

Joyce was to draw on the Maamtrasna trials again in *Finnegan's Wake,* In it we are told that "little headway, if any, was made in solving the wasnottobe crime cunundrum when a child of Maam, Festy King, of a family long and honourably associated with the tar and feather industries, who gave an address in old plomansch Mayo of the Saxons in the heart of a foulfamed potheen district was subsequently haled up at the Old Bailey on the calends of Mars, under an incompatibly framed indictment of both the counts". *(Finnegan's Wake, p. 85, 21-28).*

While during the trials, Myles Joyce is unable to defend himself because the judge or jury do not understand Irish, in *Finnegan's Wake,* we find Festy King confusing the jury by speaking English but using Irish language spelling conventions: "Pegger Festy, as soon as the outer layer of

76

stucckomuck had been removed at the request of a few live jurors, declared in a loud burst of poesy, through his Brythonic interpreter on his oath, mhuith peisth mhuise as fearra bheura muirre hriomas". *(Finnegan's Wake,* p. 91. 1-5)

Unlike the unfortunate Myles, however, "King, having murdered all the English he knew, picked out his pockets and left the tribunal scot free, trailing his Tommeyloomey's tunic in his hurry, thereinunder proudly showing off the blink pitch to his britgits to prove himself (an't plase yous!) a raelgenteel"'(Finnegan's *Wake, 93, 1-5).*

Though Joyce was by no means a nationalist he was forced in his articles for the newspapers and his lectures on Ireland to think about Ireland, its culture, its politics and its place among the nations. Nora too was thinking of Ireland and above all of Galway. Joyce had begun to write *Ulysses,* but his drinking was still a problem particularly for Nora and the two children. In May 1908 he had an attack of iritis which was so severe that he had stopped drinking for a few months.

1908 was in fact a bad year for the Joyces. Nora went through the trauma of a miscarriage on the 4th of August. Along with this and Joyce's illness, there was the continued struggle for existence. Stanislaus, in his diary for 12th September, noted that he had saved the Joyces from starvation on at least six occasions.

They were caught in a great crisis. The inevitable happened. There was a falling out with Stanislaus and Stanislaus in a huff left the Joyces to their own devices. Of course the Joyces straightaway saw their mistake and were not very slow in eating humble pie and asking Stanislaus for forgiveness and pardon. There were reconciled but they decided it was better for both brothers to live apart.

The Central Hospital, formely The Workhouse, where Nora was born.

Lower Abbeygate Street from Whitehall. Nora's first home.

Augustine Street, looking towards Whitehall. Home of Nora's grandmother.

The Convent of Mercy. Nora's school.

Date of Entrance, 18 *92*.	Register Number	Pupils' Names in Full	Age of Pupil last Birth Day.	Religious Denomination	Residence	Occupation or Means of Living of Parents	School	County	Class
Oct 14:	543	1 *Nora Bridge*	8	R.C	Nun's Island	Labourer	*transferred from*		
" "	619	2 *Mary K. Bradley*	8	"	Bohermore	*Fitt.*			
" "	639	3 *Nora Barnicle*	8	"	Prospect Hill	Baker	"		
" "	668	4 *Bridget Fahy*	7	"	College Road	Orphan			
" "	670	5 *Cissey Casey*	7	"	Bohermore	Pauper	"	"	"

Name of Pupil	Year ending	No. of Attendances made in the Year.	Class in which Enrolled.	Previous Date of Admission to this Class.	Class in which Examined.	Reading, &c.	Spelling, &c.	Writing, &c.	Arithmetic.	Grammar.	Geography.	Needlework.	Extra Branches				State whether Pupil passed or failed.	If Pupil be struck off, give date.	If Pupil be re-admitted, give date.
1 *Nora Bridge*	30.4.93			6.91	I	0	0	1	1							*fr.*	28.3.96	
	30.4.94	134	II	3/94	II	1	1	1	1		1						36. 6.97	5.7.97
	30.4.95	140	III	6/94	III	2	0	1	0	0	0	2	0				1	11.10.97
	30.4.97	126	III	6/94	III	1	1	2	1	2	1	2	2	2			20. 0. 77	
2 *Mary K. Bradley*	30.4.92	168	I	6.91	I	2	1	1	2						*fr.*		26.0.97	
	30.4.93	160	II	5/92	II	0	0	1	1						1			
	30.4.94	166	II	5/92	II	2	1	1			0							
	30.4.95	165	III	6/94	III	2	0	1	1	0	2	1	–					
	30.4.96	177	IV	6/95	IV	1	0	1	2	0	0	1	1					
	30.4.97	185	V'	5/96	V'	0	2	2	2	0	2	1	2					
3 *Nora Barnicle*	30.4.92	31	I	6.91	I	1	1	1	1						1			
	30.4.93	193	II	5/92	II	1	1	1	1						2			
	30.4.94	173	III	5/93	III	1	1	2	2	0	1							
	30.4.95	196	IV	6/94	IV	1	1	2	0	0	0	1	1					
	30.4.96	180	IV	6/94	IV	1	1	1	1	2	0	1	1					
4 *Bridget Fahy*	30.4.92	68	I	6.91	I	1	1	1	1						1		2. 4. 99	
	30.4.93	195	I	5/92	I	1	0	1	1			2						
	30.4.94	190	II	5/93	II	1	1	2	0	2	2	0						
	30.4.95	190	III	"	III	1	0	1	1	2	1	2	1					
	30.4.96	185	IV	6/95	IV	1	1	1	2	0	0	2	1					
	30.4.97	158	V'	5/96	V'	0	0	2	1	0	0	0	2					
	30.4.98	128	V'	5/96	V'	1	2	2	3	0	1	2	0					
	30.4.99	108	V²	6.98	V²	0	2	0	0	2	0	2						
5 *Cissey Casey*	30.4.92	107	I			1	1	1	1						1	*struck*		

Nora's School Record as shown in Mercy Convent Register

Presentation Convent where Nora worked as porteress.

8 BOWLING GREEN
HOME OF
NORA BARNACLE.

Eyre Square with No. 2 Prospect Hill in background, Home of Michael Bodkin.

"Can your friend in the soda water factory write my verses"

Regatta Day Menlo Castle

CHAPTER 4

THE GALWAY VISITS

During 1909, Joyce was to revisit Ireland for the first time. In March of that year, the Joyces changed lodgings and Joyce got positive support from one of his pupils, Ettore Schmitz. In July, he received payment in advance for a year's lessons from another of his pupils and this allowed him the opportunity of visiting Dublin for the first time in nearly five years.

He took with him Giorgio and for the next six weeks renewed his acquaintance with his many friends. In the back of his mind lay the hope that he would see his book *Dubliners* published and then apply for a professorship of Romance Languages in the new National University which was emerging in place of the Royal University. Joyce and Giorgio arrived in Dublin on the 29th July 1909 where they were received with open arms by his sisters but rather coldly by his father who always resented his elopement as putting an end to a promising literary career.

Joyce wrote Nora a postcard telling her they had arrived safely. He addressed it to Nora Barnacle Joyce. This in fact was his answer to the question put to him constantly by family and friends, "how do we address Nora?"

On the 6th August, the world collapsed around him in his native city. He was walking with a college friend, Vincent Cosgrave, discussing their young days when suddenly Cosgrave boasted that while Joyce was courting Nora in the summer of 1904 he too was courting her on the alternate evenings. The truth, of course, was that he had tried to court her and win her from Joyce but had been rejected.

Joyce was in a stupor. His anger turned on Nora. She had not told him the whole story of her life. She was dishonest. She was faithless. With time to think and brood he began to wonder was it he or Cosgrave was the father of Giorgio. Within an hour of his conversation with Cosgrave he wrote a troubled disturbed letter to Nora in Trieste.

"Nora I am not going to Galway nor is Georgie.

I am going to throw up the business I came for and which I hoped would have bettered my position.

I have been frank in what I have told you of myself. You have not been so with me.

At the time when I used to meet you at the corner of Merrion Square and walk out with you and feel your hand touch me in the dark and hear your voice (O, Nora ! I will never hear that music again because I can never believe again) at the time I used to meet you, every second night you kept an appointment with a friend of mine outside the Museum, you went with him along the same streets, down by the canal, past the 'house with the upstairs in it', down to the bank of the Dodder. You stood with him: he put his arms around you and you lifted your face and kissed him. What else did you do together? And the next night you met me!"

(Letters 11, 231-232)

The letter continues in a tone of anguish, lamenting his lost love and repeatedly asking Nora to write to him.

It was the letter of a jealous lover. There is nothing like jealousy to rekindle a faltering love. Many times during the years 1904-1909 Joyce was unsure of his love of Nora, but now that he thought another had come between them his love for Nora burst forth with all its first-love force. With time to recall the summer of 1904 and to brood over the treachery of Nora he wrote to her on the 7th August 1909 "Is Georgie my son?".

Joyce now decided to cut short his visit to Ireland and return to Trieste broken-hearted. Luckily he met his friend, John F. Byrne at 7 Eccles Street. Byrne suspected that Cosgrave was imagining his relationship with Nora and that there was a plot between Cosgrave and Oliver Gogarty to destroy Joyce's spirit as they feared he would belittle them

79

in his writings. Thus Byrne consoled Joyce and assured him "it was a blasted lie".

Meanwhile Nora was very upset on receiving Joyce's letters from Dublin. She felt abandoned and betrayed and had no one to speak to or confide in except Stanislaus. Stanislaus, in fact, was an unexpected source of comfort. Richard Ellmann records now, in 1904, Cosgrave had confided in Stanislaus his failure to win Nora from Joyce, and had sworn him to secrecy. In these new circumstances, Stanislaus was able to break his silence and to help Nora understand the background of Joyce's recent letters.

Nora allowed Joyce to cool his heels before she answered his letters. This she did with marvellous dignity. She felt that because she was an unlettered girl she was in no way suitable or acceptable as a companion or 'wife' for a university graduate who had written poetry and prose and who spoke a greal deal about becoming one day a world famous artist. She argued that it would be better that she stand aside from the onward march of this great man and not impede him in any way. So in answering his letter she offered just that: let Joyce forget about her and separate from her and she would make her way through life with their two children placed safely in a children's home.

By the time Nora's letter to Joyce arrived in Dublin Joyce had Stanislaus's assurance of Nora's absolute loyalty and fidelity to him in standing against Cosgrave in 1904. This assurance resurrected his former love for Nora. It deepened and strengthened that love and never again did he doubt or question her faithfulness and loyalty. He regretted beyond words that she should ever have doubted her and he wrote her on the 19th August an abject apology. "My sweet noble Nora, I ask you to forgive me for my contemptible conduct... forgive me sweetheart won't you?..... don't read over these horrible letters I wrote. I was out of my mind with rage at the time.... Nora darling, I apologise to you humbly".

On the 22nd August 1909 he wrote a letter to Nora full of love and hope. He recognised that their love had come through a great crisis and that even though they suffered much in that moment the future was full of promise and happiness. "What can come between us now? we have suffered and been tried. Every veil of shame or diffidence seems to have fallen down on us. Will we not see in each other's eyes the hours and hours of happiness that are waiting for us?..... Do you remember the three adjectives I have used in *The Dead* in speaking of your body? They are these 'musical and strange and perfumed'.... Do not let me ever lose the love I have for you now Nora".

Joyce now had visiting cards printed and represented himself as a reporter of the Triestine paper *Piccolo della Sera*'. The Press pass enabled Joyce and Giorgio to travel by train free to Galway. It was the 26th August 1909. The purpose of the visit was allegedly to write some articles about Galway for the paper, but in reality it was to visit Nora's family and attempt a reconciliation.

Like many a brave man he found the last few steps of his journey the hardest. He stood at the corner of Lombard Street and Bowling Green and wondered how Mrs Annie Barnacle might receive him. He sent Giorgio, then aged almost four years, to No. 4, Bowling Green where the Barnacles lived to announce the arrival of the Joyces.

In truly grandmother style Annie Barnacle hugged young Giorgio and then received Joyce with open arms. Joyce found that Annie Barnacle was very like her daughter Nora. Immediately they were friends and found it very easy to stay in one another's company. The result was that Joyce spent most of his stay in Galway in the kitchen of No. 4 Bowling Green while Giorgio amused himself chasing hens and ducks up and down Bowling Green.

Joyce explored Galway with Nora's sister Kathleen as guide. He went to St. Augustine Street/Whitehall to see the house and room where Nora lived with her grandmother Mrs. Healy. He walked with Kathleen Barnacle on the strand at Grattan Road and enjoyed the sweep of the Atlantic, washing the shore at the edge of Galway Bay.

Joyce visited the memorial to Mayor Lynch in Market

81

Street with its crossbones and skull and following inscription:

> "This memorial of the stern and unbending justice of the chief magistrate of this city, James Lynch Fitzstephen, Elected Mayor A.D. 1493, who condemned and executed his own guilty son, Walter on this spot, has been restored to its ancient site A.D. 1854 with the approval of the Town Commissioners by their chairman, Very Rev. Peter Daly, P.P."

Most of Joyce's time was spent with Mrs. Barnacle and he got her to sing for him 'The Lass of Aughrim' which he had so often heard sung by Nora, and which in *"The Dead"* sparked off Gretta's memories of Michael Furey. Mrs Barnacle's version was more complete. It is a sad song in which the unmarried Lass of Aughrim is disowned by her lover Lord Gregory and sadly the lass drowns herself.

There were, in fact, a number of verses, which Mrs Barnacle refused to sing. In these, Lord Gregory asks the Lass of Aughrim for a token of their love:-

> "Oh, if you be the lass of Aughrim
> As I suppose you not to be
> Come tell me the last token
> Between you and me.
>
> O Gregory, don't you remember
> One night on the hill
> When we swapped rings of each other's hands
> Sorely against my will?
> Mine was of beaten gold
> Yours was but block tin."

Joyce wrote a letter-card to Nora "sitting at the kitchen table in your mother's house'. In it he expressed the wish that "next year you and I may come here". Mrs Barnacle noticed that Joyce was sighing openly and deeply so much did he miss Nora and she softly chided him that unless he was sensible he would 'break his heart at it'. Nora's uncle, Michael Healy, a Custom's Official gave Joyce and Giorgio room and bed in his house in Dominick Street the two nights they stayed in Galway.

On the 31st August 1909, Joyce was back in Dublin. He wrote a most tender letter to Nora and bought an expensive gift to give her in Trieste. "I would wish you to be surrounded by everything that is fine" he wrote her. "You are not as you say, a poor uneducated girl. You are my bride, darling and all I can give you of pleasure and joy in this life I wish to give you......... our children (much as I love them) must not come between us".

Joyce himself designed the present for Nora. It was a gold chain with cubes of ivory. Inscribed on one side of the main piece of ivory was "love is unhappy" and on the other side "when love is away" a quotation from one of his poems. The chain and ivories were enclosed in a brown letter case and there was a card inserted with the inscription in gold lettering "Nora 1904-1909".

The crisis Joyce had been through went deeper than was at first evident and it revealed in him feelings and thoughts that were strange to him. Images of Nora in every kind of pose and posture tormented him "grotesque, shameful, virginal, langourous". He wrote to Nora "tonight I have an idea madder than usual. I feel I would like to be flogged by you.......... I wonder is there some madness in me°or is love madness?" He wrote impassioned letters to Nora and all the time the central theme and thought is sexual "Oh take me into your soul of souls' ...."Oh how I long to feel your body mingled with mine".

Joyce and Giorgio sailed from Dublin to return to Trieste and to Nora on the 9th September 1909. His sister Eva accompanied them. Nora had asked Joyce to being her along in the hope that she would act as baby-sitter and being religious minded that she might have some influence on Joyce. Eva was fairly skilled in dressmaking and it was hoped she would easily find suitable work in Trieste.

The changed Joyce arrived at Trieste on the 13th September 1909. It was an eventful journey punctuated by stops at London and Paris. In Paris he had to fish his ring, a present from Nora, out of the toilet bowl. He eventually found it at the bottom of a drain. Nora to her credit gave Joyce a warm welcome on his belated return. She had spruced herself for the occasion. She had set her hair and she looked young and girlish as she received Joyce as a long lost lover. Joyce was tired after the journey and retired to bed. Later Nora wakened him from his reverie and here they confronted one another as bride and bridegroom in the bridal suite.

But Joyce, despite his many protestations of love in his letters from Dublin to Nora was profligate. The result was that Nora was surly and rude to Joyce and when Joyce came home drunk she turned her back on him and refused all approaches.

Eva Joyce was fascinated by the two cinemas in Trieste. It was she, in fact, who gave Joyce the idea of establishing a cinema or cinemas in Dublin, which idea was to give him the opportunity of visiting Dublin again.

Joyce was thrilled with the idea and he quickly persuaded two Triestians to sponsor him. Joyce signed a contract to go to Ireland and find sites for cinemas in Dublin, Cork and Belfast. The sponsors allowed him expenses of ten crowns a day and one tenth of the profits.

He set out from Trieste on the 18th October 1909, a little more than a month after his return from Dublin. A few minutes before his departure Nora who was embittered by his drinking and carousing stood before Joyce and called him "an imbecile". The remark struck home and hurt Joyce as it was intended to. Joyce, intentionally, for once allowed her to cool her heels and did not write to Nora for a whole week. His letter to her of the 25th October, is full of apologies and proclamations of love and promises of gifts and presents. He blurts out to her "I shall never be tired of you, dearest, if you will only be a little more polite........ you are my only love..... you have me completely in your power."

Nora was not fully consoled by these letters from Dublin. She doubted his fidelity and loyalty and felt miserable. She wrote to him telling him she was sure he was tired of her. Immediately he replied assuring her of his love. "Nora I love you, I cannot live without you..... bear with me if I am inconsiderate and unmanageable...... let me love you in my own way....... You are a sad little person and I am a devilishly melancholy fellow myself so that ours is a rather mournful love I fancy".

But while it was wonderful to get such assurances of loyalty and love, Nora was left penniless in Trieste with two children and no source of income except the generosity of Stanislaus. In mid-November, the process server came to her door with a writ for the rent for October and November on pain of immediate eviction. Stanislaus cabled Joyce in Dublin but the support of Joyce's father and his sisters had fallen on Joyce and there was nothing he could send to Trieste to relieve the anguish of his wife and children.

On Christmas Eve 1909, he wired a little, very little money to Nora in Trieste, otherwise she was abandoned to the charity of Stanislaus and the fragments from the tables of the concerned neighbours. All this time Joyce wrote to Nora almost daily and Nora in turn wrote to him. While in Dublin he developed attacks of sciatica and then iritis and concluded it was the Dublin damp and cold. So as soon as he got a licence for the Volta Cinema in Dublin he braced himself to return to Trieste.

On the 2nd January 1910, he left Dublin. This time he took with him his sister Eileen aged 21 hoping that she would help Nora with the household chores and hopefully have her voice trained, as she was a promising soprano. On his return to Trieste Joyce was confined to bed for a whole month to rest his eyes. By February 1910, Joyce was up and about and able to give English lessons to his pupils once again. For the rest of 1910 and during 1911, life went on much as usual. Nora, now surrounded by Joyces, found herself in the middle of family squabbles, both petty and open. For one period Joyce and Stanislaus would only exchange letters. Once or twice Stanislaus left vowing never to return and in July 1911, Eva left for Dublin disgusted with the whole set-up.

Once, in dire straits, Nora wrote to Galway saying she was returning to Bowling Green, but it was only a threat, and she tore up the letter.

1911 ground slowly into 1912. The Joyce family lived on from hand to mouth barely keeping the rent-man from the door. Meanwhile Joyce, trying to improve his position dreamed of getting an appointment as a teacher in an Italian public school. In April 1912, he sat for an examination in Padua. He passed with honours. But the Italian Department of Education refused to accept his Royal University B.A., as a valid degree and so he could not teach.

Early 1912 Nora began to correspond with her family in Galway. Absence made the heart grow fonder and she was filled with a great desire to see her family. At last early in July Nora set off for Ireland and Galway. She took her daughter Lucia with her. She hoped when she arrived in Galway to extract some money from her bachelor uncle Michael Healy to enable Joyce and Giorgio to join her there.

Before she departed she discussed with Joyce the embarrassment which she would suffer in her home town if she did not wear a marriage ring. Joyce wished that she be honest and straightforward about their 'marriage' and forbade her to wear a ring. But Nora had her own plans and ignored Joyce's pleas and orders. She took a ring with her.

They arrived in Dublin on Monday, 8th July. They were met at Westland Row by all the Joyce family then in Dublin. John Joyce, was charmed to meet Nora for the first time and he was completely overcome on seeing his granddaughter Lucia. He brought Nora and Lucia for a meal to Finn's Hotel in celebration.

On the following day Nora called to the publisher Roberts at Joyce's request to press for the publication of *Dubliners* which had been in his hands for some years now. John Joyce and his son Charles accompanied her on her visit to Roberts. This was unfortunate as they adopted a hostile attitude towards Roberts and Roberts refused to be rushed into any sudden decision.

About the 12th July, Nora and Lucia arrived in Galway. At Galway station she was rather apprehensive as the train came to a halt as she was unsure of the welcome she would receive from her mother and family. She was overwhelmed with the warmth of her reception. Her mother smothered her with welcome and love.

All the neighbours flocked into Bowling Green to meet the girl who had married 'the writer Joyce' as her mother had often told them. Lucia, of course, was the centre of all attention and of many compliments. Nora's uncle, Michael Healy offered her accommodation in his home in Dominick Street and here she retired each night during her stay in Galway.

Michael Healy had just had a spell in hospital having surgical treatment for his nose and had spent a "bucket full of money" in getting a superfluous bone removed. Thus he had not now the plentiness of money which the Joyces had imagined as they dreamed their dreams in Trieste.

When Lucia was tucked into bed one night Nora wrote a tender note to Joyce in Trieste. "My darling Jim, since I left Trieste I am continually thinking about you. How are you getting on without me or do you miss me at all? I am dreadfully lonely for you. I am quite tired of Ireland already."

In the meantime Joyce felt lonely and piqued because Nora had not within a day written a letter to him assuring him of her love. In this fit of pique he left Trieste with Giorgio and followed Nora to Ireland. It was his third time in three years and the last visit of his life.

After a few days in Dublin Joyce set off for Galway to be with Nora and their children. In Galway/he began to live a full life of peace and happiness. He was sure of his meals and there were no threats of eviction, although the shadow of eviction from their flat in Trieste hung over them all the time. In a letter to Stanislaus dated 7th August 1912, Joyce wrote "tell Bartoli I have a lot of news re transatlantic scheme and to see my second article on Aran. I think since I have come so far I had better stay a little longer if possible. Nora's uncle feeds us in great style and I row and cycle and drive a good deal. I cycled to Oughterard on Sunday and visited the graveyard of *The Dead*. It is exactly as I imagined it and one of the headstones was to J. Joyce......."

For three weeks Nora and Joyce enjoyed themselves in Galway. They sported on the strand in Salthill and Grattan Road. They sailed to Aran Islands in one or other of the two ships that sailed four times each week from Galway Docks to the Aran Islands. The Durus was the older ship, being then near the end of her tether. The Dun Aengus was span new and so was more comfortable and seaworthy. The return fare for cabin passengers was 4/6 and for passengers on the open deck was 3/6.

During these weeks, Joyce wrote two articles in Italian – one about Galway, and one about the Aran Islands for the *Piccolo della Sera.*

The article on Galway is called "The City of the Tribes: Italian Echoes in an Irish Port". He talks about the Spanish influence on the architecture on the town, but not on the complexion of its people. He sees Galway as being the Spanish city "in the twilight of its history". He talks of the history of Galway and its great European trade, the signs of which can be still seen in the street names such as Madeira Street, Merchant Street, Spaniards Walk, Madeira Island, Lombard Street, Velasquez de Palmeira Boulevard.

The article continues in this vein giving some Italian connections with the city. He talks about the tribes, and Henry Joyce who prepared a map of the city for Charles 11 of England. Joyce then launches into the legend of Lynch's Castle from which the Mayor of Galway James Lynch Fitzstephen is said to have hung his son Walter for the murder of a Spaniard called Gomez.

The article is highly coloured, written for an Italian audience, but in the last paragraph, Joyce paints a strangely evocative and somewhat domestic scene:

"The evening is quiet and grey. From the distance, beyond the waterfall, comes a murmur. It sounds like the hum of bees around a hive. It comes closer. Six young men appear, playing bagpipes, at the head of a band of people. They pass, proud and warlike, with heads uncovered, playing a vague and strange music. In the uncertain light you can hardly distinguish the green plaids hanging from the right shoulder and the saffron-coloured kilts. They enter the street of the Convent of Offerings, and, as the vague music spreads in the twilight, at the windows of the convent appear, one by one, the white veils of the nuns."

(James Joyce Critical Writings, Viking Press, New York, pp 233)

The second article — "The Mirage of the Fisherman of Aran: England's Safety Valve in Case of War" — begins with a description of the blessing of the Bay and the Claddagh fishing fleet every 15th of August. Joyce relates this to the Spanish Armada and the protection the citizens of Galway gave to its shipwrecked sailors.

Joyce then speaks of the advantages of Galway as a transatlantic port. He talks of Christopher Columbus as being the last to discover America. St. Brendan had done so a thousand years before him. Both left from America from the Aran Islands.

On reaching the island, Joyce talks of the nimbleness of the islanders, their clothes, their turn of phrase, their imagination, inherent nobility, poverty, and impulsive hospitality. On the return journey a steady drizzle falls and the islands disappear, a little mystically, "wrapped in a smoky veil".

On his return from the Aran Islands, Joyce pondered a little more on the idea of establishing a transatlantic port in Galway Bay. Nothing was more calculated to raise the hopes and dreams of the people of the city than the establishment of a transatlantic port. The distance saved by sailing from Galway to America over any other port in Great Britain is so considerable, that Galway with its safe natural harbour had outstanding claims to being named a transatlantic port.

In 1850 an attempt was first made to establish a packet station in Galway which would convey the mail under contract to America. The Railway Company gave £500 towards the undertaking and several businessmen backed the effort and in due time the steamship, Viceroy of Dublin, sailed from Galway carrying 'Her Majesty's Mails'. It carried 1,120 letters and 33 passengers. The Viceroy reached Halifax in nine days. On the return journey the Viceroy ran aground on a small island approximately 130 miles out from Halifax and to this day the Galway people believe that the pilot was bribed to wreck it lest Galway should oust Liverpool as the important link between England and America.

In 1858 Mr. Lever of Liverpool proposed to start a transatlantic line between Galway and America. The first vessel announced to sail in the Lever Line was the 'Indian Empire' with accommodation for 1,000 passengers. Alas, the 'Indian Empire' with two skilful pilots aboard, picked up off Aran, on a clear tranquil night struck the only obstacle in the nine mile wide bay, the San Marguerite Rock and was wrecked. At subsequent investigations the two pilots were found guilty of a deliberate attempt to run the ship aground.

Joyce was a shrewd judge of the potentialities of the Bay. Yet because of his absolute penury his scheme of making it a transatlantic port could never be more than a dream.

One day Joyce went to Clifden by train with the intention of interviewing the great Marconi and writing an article on him and his radio station for the Italian Press. He was unlucky in the trip as Marconi was out of town just then.

Marconi was a pioneer in the radio business. As early as January 1903, on his wireless station a message transmitted by President Roosevelt from the radio station at South Wellfleet Massachussets was received and answered by King Edward V11 at Poldhu in Cornwall. Marconi later chose Clifden for a radio station because it provided the shortest link with the Marconi Station on Cape Breton island across the Atlantic. Construction of Clifden station began in October 1905. The steam driven power had an output of 300 kilowatts, the boilers being fired with turf. The station was opened in 1907 and was the first point to point fixed wireless service in the world.

Joyce and Nora walked up to Terryland on Sunday 20th July, to sit by the River Corrib and watch the crews strive for victory at the Annual Galway Regatta, always a popular outing for lovers of boating on the river. The Regatta is still a feature of Galway sport life. Joyce took Nora to the Galway Races on Wednesday and Thursday, 7th and 8th August and they enjoyed them immensely. The Galway Races even then were a festival where country men rubbed shoulders with 'townies'.

The weather was warm and kind, though there were one or two slight showers. One thing irked Joyce as he watched the gentry besporting themselves on the stands. He felt that Nora and he rightly deserved to be there in their midst as befitted a world class author. He hoped that the day would come when he would be able to give Nora the fame she deserved and he promised that they would yet take their rightful place in the enclosure with the upper class.

Noble Grecian, the top weight at 12 st. 5 won the Galway Plate, being returned at 4/1. The odds scarcely mattered to our friends, as they were actually penniless and could only enjoy the things that were free. They were free too to stand outside the Railway Hotel in Eyre Square and look with envious eyes at the country gentlemen and ladies as they gathered there for the Annual Race Ball.

On the 17th August 1912, Joyce left Galway for Dublin leaving Nora with their two children in Galway.He hoped to get his book, *Dubliners*, printed by Roberts but found himself double crossed by his solicitor and Roberts. Nora sent him a telegram of encouragement "Courage Angelo Mio".

In a letter to Nora on the 21st August in which he is rather muddled and puzzled he expressed his deep love for Nora.

"I should like.... to take you about during the Horse Show". Once again he tells her of his grief at Galway Races. "I feel it still, I hope that the day may come when I shall be able to give you the fame of being beside me."

Further he disclosed to her that he had had a long conversation with his aunt about her. He listed some of the peculiarities of Nora: how she sat at the opera with the grey ribbon in her hair and how she listened to the music observed by men.

On the 22nd August, Joyce wrote to Nora and asked her to join him in Dublin. He had rented a double-bedded room on the North Circular Road. "I wish you were here. You have become a part of myself — one flesh. The Abbey Theatre will be open and they will give plays of Yeats and Synge. You have a right to be there because you are my bride."

This was a disheartening time for Nora. Joyce kept her informed from Dublin of the annoying objections to the printing of his book, *Dubliners.* The sheets of the book were indeed printed but the publisher and printer then burned them. She had to suffer all the embarrassment of her husband's failure as she was being supported and comforted by her family in Galway so when Joyce called her to Dublin she was happy to go to escape embarrassment.

Her stay in the flat in the North Circular Road was short as the money Joyce expected from the publication of *Dubliners* did not accrue and the Joyce family was forced to accept the hospitality of Joyce's uncle, William Murray and his wife Josephine.

Here on the 25th August, brother Stanislaus sent a telegram from Trieste "Come without delay". As Dublin and Ireland had now nothing to offer them they were disconsolate. Mrs Murray one evening prepared a special meal for them to cheer them up. When all was ready for the meal Joyce went upstairs to the piano to sing a love song. His behaviour embarrassed Nora beyond words and she showed it. Mrs Murray consoled Nora and told her "ah, do go up to him! Can't you see, all that is for you".

Nothing else mattered for Joyce at that moment except his love for Nora and at the piano he poured out his soul to her and she to him. In their great distress they said goodbye to the Murrays and left Dublin on the 11th September 1912. After stops in London and Flushing they reached Trieste on the 15th September.

For a year, after their return to Trieste, the Joyces struggled against poverty. Towards the end of 1913, however, a gradual change came over Joyce's financial position. The publisher Grant Richards asked to look at *Dubliners*. Ezra Pound, the American poet, wanted anything Joyce had ready for publication. He was involved in several literary magazines, and was prepared to publish Joyce.

Finally on the 15th June 1914, *Dubliners* appeared. Reviews were generally favourable, but not enthusiastic. Nora wasn't greatly interested in either the publication or the reviews, but was pleased that the genius of her husband was at last being recognized, and that there was a promise of fairer days ahead.

About this time, Joyce became infatuated with one of his pupils, Amalia Popper. He never, however, approached her overtly and his infatuation soon passed, though her image haunted him for some years.

The outbreak of World War 1 had little immediate effect on Joyce and Nora. Stanislaus, however, was interned for its duration as being hostile to Austria. When Italy entered the war, the scene changed and the Joyces thought it prudent to move to neutral Switzerland. They returned to Zurich. Zurich presented some problems to Nora – not the least of which was the language – but, in general, she was happy there and its character and charm appealed to her. While there were still financial worries, the burden was gradually easing. In times of crisis, Michael Healy of Galway was always helpful. Joyce managed to secure some pupils and was receiving gifts of money from admirers. Also, in London, Ezra Pound prevailed upon Yeats to get Joyce a grant from the Royal Literary Fund, the Civil List and the

Society of Authors.

Despite all the difficulties of war, exile and language, 1916 was a happy and most successful year for the Joyces. This happiness exuded in a letter Joyce wrote to Yeats on the 14th September, thanking him for having secured a literary grant of £100 for Joyce. Acceptable as this money was to the Joyces what really thrilled them was that "it was a sign of recognition". Now they forgot all the years of hardship, frustration, "betrayals", and with a full heart Joyce could say, "I have been very grateful to the many friends who have helped me".

With the easing of the financial problems, medical ones began to appear. Joyce's eyes began to give trouble and, towards the end of 1916, he suffered from depression and nervousness. Early in 1917, he had a severe attack of glaucoma and, because of complications, he was laid up for over a month.

During the summer of 1917, the Joyces found the Zurich climate to be unhealthy and exacting, and the doctor advised them to move to Locarno where the weather was milder. Nora and the children did so immediately, but Joyce had to remain in Zurich because of his eyes. Nora wrote back to Joyce that Locarno was pleasant. Ironically, perhaps, the people appealed to her because they were "just like Italians, lively, dirty and disorderly".

On the 18th of August, Joyce suffered a severe attack of glaucoma and had to be operated on. Nora rushed back to Zurich to be with him. The operation, though successful, reduced his vision, and it was October before he was well enough to travel to Locarno.

Joyce's health improved in Locarno and he wrote quite a lot. But he gradually became bored and restless. This boredom was reflected in the home by silence. Nora was to say of this period, "Jim never spoke to me at the Pension Daheim". To add to her discomfort, the children became sickly. So, after only a few months, the Joyce family returned to Zurich, to their crowded cafes and friends.

Around this time, the Joyces became very involved in the

theatre. They went to plays frequently, locking the children securely in their rooms, and thus dispensing with babysitters The children resented this, and often shouted after them from the windows but, as they spoke in Italian, nobody understood them.

Joyce became interested in producing plays and, with Claud Sykes, an English actor, formed a company of English players. One of the plays produced in 1918 was Synge's *Riders to the Sea*. Nora, because of her fine figure and her rich west of Ireland accent, was persuaded to play the part of Cathleen the daughter of the bereaved Maura. Joyce trained the other actors to imitate her accent and the play was a smash hit, with Nora playing superbly.

One of the part time actors of the company was Frank Budgen. He was to become one of Joyce's closest friends, and they had many protracted drinking bouts together. Nora resented this constant drinking and blamed Budgen for it. One night, after Joyce had quarrelled with Nora about him, Budgen invited her to join them. She did and they in turn became quite friendly.

Budgen admired Nora's qualities and treated her with great respect. In his book *Myselves when Young*, written some fifty years later, he describes how one night he was walking in Nora's company with Joyce just behind. Nora became quite tearful and told Budgen that Joyce wanted her to go with other men so he would have something to write about. Budgen continues, "That Nora would or could have co-operated in any such way is out of the question. She was a respectable married woman with all that implies and any such enterprise lay outside her will and means."

Joyce was working very hard on *Ulysses*. Nora was completely indifferent to his writing — an indifference which somewhat bewildered Joyce. He would read a paragraph or two to her, but she could not enthuse over it. She found the language unacceptable and failed to see any value in it.

Nora was more than a match for Joyce. She sometimes treated him as a child, and she remained completely independent of him. He confessed this to Budgen:- "I have an effect of some kind on people who come near me and know me and who are my friends. But my wife's personality is absolute proof against any influence of mine."

In his biography, Richard Ellmann sees this as the very reason why Nora suited Joyce. "She endured her husband's erratic life as graciously as possible," he says, "and endeavoured only to moderate his frailities".

About this time, Joyce became infatuated with another woman, Martha Fleischmann. It may have been that she symbolized for Joyce the girl he had seen on Sandymount Strand in 1898 and who reappeared in *Ulysses*. Nora was aware of the infatuation: it ruffled her, but did not upset her.

Towards the end of 1919, the Joyce odyssey began again. They left Zurich in October and returned to Trieste. But Trieste had lost all the qualities that had appealed to them before the war, and their stay there was only for nine months. Joyce thought of returning to Ireland for a short while but fear of being shot – this was the period of "The Troubles" – and lack of money made the venture impossible.

In July 1920, the Joyces left Trieste and, with stops at Venice, Milan and Dijon, arrived in Paris on the 8th. They found Paris warm and pleasant despite language difficulties and financial problems.

The Joyce children were now teenagers. They had been reared as citizens of no country. The had no language, no home, and this was reflected in a crisis of identity. They were both influenced more by Joyce than by Nora, but he made no attempt to mould or discipline them.

Giorgio was fifteen. He was a strapping six foot with certain athletic prowess. He was finished with schooling and was unemployed.

Lucia was thirteen, handsome, vivacious and a little precocious. She found it hard to reconcile the home poverty with the social life of her parents and was, even then, beginning to develop a split personality. She had visions of carving out a career for herself as an artist, and was to try various media. But that was in the future. Now, in 1920 in Paris, she was once again trying to adjust to a new language, a new coterie of visitors, and new friends.

For the first two years in Paris, life was a mixture of struggles and success. The Joyces were practically always poor, but Joyce himself was the centre of adulation in literary circles. *Ulysses* was being prepared for publication, but Joyce suffered from periodic attacks on his eyes from neuralgia. Through all of this Nora was mother, nurse and wife. While finishing *Ulysses*, Joyce was leaning more and more on the bottle. Nora once again took him in hand and disciplined him. She accompanied him on his social evenings and was always able to get him home. When others stood in awe of him, she had his measure. While others paid court to him, she brought him down to earth calling him a "good for nothing". She often chaffed him regretting that she hadn't married a farmer or a banker.

On the 2nd February 1922, Joyces 40th birthday, Sylvia Beach, an American, then running a shop in Paris under the name Shakespeare and Company published *Ulysses*. It was a red letter day that they had for so long been looking forward to. The first three copies of the edition, in Grecian blue paper with white lettering were rushed from Dijon to Paris by express train. To celebrate the historic occasion the Joyces brought their friends to an Italian cafe where Joyce untied his copy of *Ulysses* and laid it on the table.

It was an historic night and the Joyces were feted and one of the guests proposed a toast to the book. Joyce would gladly have spent the night in revelry but Nora knowing the risks and dangers to his health talked him into going home.

Joyce inscribed the first copy of the book which Sylvia Beach brought to him, to his wife Nora. She was not in the least impressed. Indeed, she offered to sell it and worse still she refused to read it. The critics and reviewers were divided down the middle as to what to say about *Ulysses*. Some saw it as a satire on modern life, a brilliant one at that, others saw it as an obscene joke. Perhaps Nora's critique was the most realistic "I guess the man's a genius, but what a dirty mind he has, hasn't he".

Joyce celebrated his success by frequenting bistros until late at night and often till late morning when he returned home blind drunk. Invariably Nora helped him out of the taxi and to bed. On one occasion Nora lost her temper and upbraided him in her best style "Jim you've been doin' this for twenty years and I'm telling you it's the end. Do you understand? You've been bringing drunken companions to me too long".

In March 1922, Nora suggested that they go back to Ireland and visit their parents and let the children see their grandparents again. They could now afford to travel as with royalties from his book and gifts from his admirers they could be considered a fairly wealthy family. Joyce was in no way in favour of visiting Ireland. As he saw it there was grave danger of Civil War in Ireland. But Nora was adamant. Come hell or high water she was going to Ireland to visit her family and to call on Joyce's family. Joyce took issue with Nora; he got angry and cross with her. They shouted their heads off in argument. Nora won.

On the 1st April 1922, Nora set off for Ireland taking with her Giorgio and Lucia. That morning Joyce pleaded with her once more to stay. Nora faced him and threatened that she would never return to him: she would live in Ireland in peace and happiness. Joyce was so anxious for his family's safety that he once more gave up the drink. He decided that he would play his last card; he would stop their journey in London. He held them up for a whole ten days by sending them telegrams and urgent letters. Again and again he appealed to them to return. He poured a string of curses on Ireland and on everyone living there. Nora eventually got tired of it all and with her children she suddenly left for Ireland. They were met in Dublin by Joyce's father and Nora's uncle Michael Healy who was then working in Dublin. They were received with open arms and evident joy.

The following day they journeyed on to Galway and hastened to Bowling Green to see Nora's mother, sisters and neighbours. The house in Bowling Green, with just one bedroom and kitchen, was too small to keep the three visitors and so they had to look for lodgings in a quiet safe area of the town.

The town was in the throes of Civil War in April 1922. The signing of the Treaty between the Irish Free State and England on December 6th 1921 soon divided the people of Ireland into two totally opposed groups, the Treatyites and the Anti-Treatyites. The Dail debated the terms of the treaty and voted on its terms. The Provisional Government was installed on January 16th. Evacuation of the British troops from the twenty-six counties began at once.

In February 1922, the Galway battalion of the I.R.A. took over the military and police installations in Galway city. Commandant Sean Turke marched an advance party of 30 to Renmore Barracks. All the English officers were there. Sean halted his men in the barrack square, put them at ease and ordered Sergeant John Kinnevane to take over the first guard. He ordered Sergeant Stephen King to pick his assistants to hoist the National Flag. He brought his group to attention once more, saluted the English officers who then departed. Then Johnny Broderick marched up with the full Battalion Company. Lenaboy Castle, home of the auxiliaries, was also vacated and taken over by the freedom fighters. Soon the I.R.A. was becoming two armies. Divisions and Brigades were divided right down the middle.

In Galway the Anti-Treaty I.R.A. were in possession of Renmore Barracks while the Pro-Treaty I.R.A. had its headquarters in the Railway Hotel in Eyre Square under Austin Brennan. From here they controlled the city, the railway terminal and the movement of people. They paraded the streets, held up people and searched them. It was a siege situation.

Nora found lodgings in Nun's Island in Casey's house. Each day she brought Giorgio and Lucia to Bowling Green to visit her mother. The young teenagers did not at all relish these visits. Mrs. Donnellan who lived next door to Mrs. Barnacle remembers these visits. Giorgio and Lucia refused to enter the home of their grandmother because they were upset by the smell of boiling cabbage coming from the house. Nora pleaded with them and Nora's sisters Delia and Kathleen begged them to go in but they sat on the windowsill and stubbornly refused to go in. Nora was very upset by their lack of nature for their own flesh and blood and was compelled to take them to a cafe for their meals.

Nora's dreams of a pleasant holiday in Galway were shattered. Her visions of setting up home there were cruelly undermined. She did take time to visit the Presentation Convent where she worked as a teenager and proudly introduced her children to the Superioress, Mother Alphonsus, with whom she exchanged Christmas cards for many years afterwards. They visited the grave of her father, Thomas Barnacle, in Rahoon cemetery.

Thomas on his retiral from the bakery business lived apart from Mrs. Barnacle, in Mary Street. He suffered quite a lot from rheumatism and in July 1921 he was removed to the Union Hospital in the Workhouse where he died on the 13th July 1921 aged 75. His wife bore the full expense of burying him. Nora may have brought her children from the grave of their grandfather to the vault-tomb of her first lover and there whispered a prayer for Michael Bodkin.

In her mother's house she would have heard all the family gossip she had missed over the years. How her brother Tom, who had a good job as a conductor in the Galway Tram Company, had emigrated to England and had not been heard of. She would have laughed at the story of her sister Delia and the Fleming boy in St. Bridget's Place in Bohermore who was courting her.

Early in 1920 curfew was declared in Galway by the Black and Tans. Anyone caught in the streets after nine o'clock was liable to be shot at or jailed. One night John Fleming was visiting his love, Delia Barnacle in Bowling Green and overstayed the time. He bravely risked the journey home across the centre of the city but alas was caught in Market Street by the Tans. They halted him and

100

questioned him about his business on the streets at such an hour. When he told them he was returning from a date with his loved one, they stripped him of his trousers, hung it on a high hook up in the wall, where a local shopkeerer usually hung dead rabbits and chickens and forced him to go back to Barnacles in the semi-nude.

Whenever Nora returned to her boarding house in Nun's Island she found Giorgio upset because again and again he had been stopped in the streets by armed men without uniforms (pro-treaty). Giorgio was a strapping lad of sixteen and a half and stood well over six feet. He was evidently, from his dress and demeanour, a stranger in the city. Consequently, he was suspect and harrassed a great deal. Breaking point came when Free State soldiers occupied Caseys boarding house, where the Joyces lodged, entered the bedrooms of the Joyces, and fired at the I.R.A. (anti-treaty) esconced in a store across the road from Caseys.

The following morning the Joyces said farewell to their friends in Galway and went to get the train back to Dublin. The train left Galway station under the protection of the Free State Army and a half mile up the line had to run the gauntlet of the I.R.A. troops at Renmore Barracks who presumed that every train into and out of Galway was against them and consequently they were against it. So they fired in the best wild west style on every train that passed the barracks and duly had pot-shots at the train the Joyces travelled in. Nora and Lucia were scared at the sound of the shootings and were frightened out of their wits. They lay down on the floor of the train "flat on their bellies". However Giorgio bravely stood his ground in the best tradition of teenage daring and effrontery.

All in all it was an inglorious exit from Nora's native city. She was never to return. Small wonder that Joyce in writing to his aunt Josephine in Dublin alluding to Nora's disappointing visit said. "No doubt you will see Nora again.. revisit her native dunghill. The air in Galway is very good but dear at the present price".

101

Uncle Michael Healy met the Joyces in Dublin as they passed through. When they told him of the shootings in Galway and the harassement they underwent he made little of it and laughed heartily at the whole episode. Nora wondered what she should do. To return to Paris meant that she was returning to Joyce with his eccentricities and problems of illness and drink. To stay in Dublin meant that she would be exposing herself and her children to all the buffeting and harassement associated with Civil War. It was Hobson's choice. She chose the 'devil she knew' and returned to Paris.

CHAPTER 5

PARIS AND THE LAST YEARS

For the next eighteen years, Joyce and Nora lived mainly in Paris. On the positive side there was Joyce's literary success and fame. This assured him financial independence and gave him the adulation he craved for.

Nora was pleased at this success, though she did not understand it. With Joyce in the spotlight, she remained very much in the shadows, an adjunct to his celebrity. For this reason, Nora's life during the twenties and thirties is seen mainly in relation to Joyce's career.

This is unfortunate, because it was during this period that Nora showed sterling qualities of love and loyalty. She nursed Joyce through his many illnesses and continued to endure his protracted drinking bouts. She watched Giorgio's singing career and marriage founder, suffered the worsening of Lucia's mental condition. She herself was to undergo one operation in 1929, but for the most part she was the stabilising rock of the Joyce family.

Sylvia Beach, publisher of *Ulysses*, recognized Nora's influence on Joyce. In her book *Shakespeare and Company*, she describes the Nora of the 1920s:-

> "Mrs Joyce was rather tall, and neither stout nor thin. She was charming, with her reddish curly hair and eyelashes, her eyes with a twinkle in them, her voice with its Irish inflections, and a certain dignity that is so Irish also".
>
> (Beach:- *Shakespeare and Company*, p. 46).

In another passage, she describes Nora's attitude to Joyce and his writing with great humour. She also tells us how essential Nora was to Joyce, even if the family did not appear to treat her seriously:-

> "Nora would have no truck with books, and that, too, amused her husband. She declared to me she hadn't read a page of "that book", pointing to *Ulysses*; nothing would induce her to open it. I

103

could see myself that it was quite unnecessary for Nora to read *Ulysses;* was she not the source of his inspiration?

Nora grumbled about "my husband"; he never stopped scribbling...... reaching down when he was only half awake in the morning for his paper and pencil on the floor beside him...... never knowing what time of day it was! And how could she keep a servant if he left the house just at the moment when she was putting lunch on the table? "Look at him now! Leeching on the bed, and scribbling away! The children too; they wouldn't lift a finger to help her" she said. "A good-for-nothing family!" Whereupon the whole good-for-nothing lot of them, including Joyce, would burst out laughing. Nobody seemed to take Nora's scoldings very seriously.

She used to tell me that she was sorry she hadn't married a farmer, or a baker, or maybe a ragpicker, instead of a writer — her lips curled as she mentioned this despicable kind of person. But what a good thing for Joyce, I thought, that she had chosen him. What would he have done without Nora? And what would his work have done without her? His marriage to Nora was one of the best pieces of luck that ever befell him. His was certainly the happiest marriage of any writer I knew".

(Beach: Id. pp. 52-53)

In early 1923, Joyce had three operations on his eyes. To recuperate it was decided to spend the summer in England and they found a quiet retreat in Bognor in Sussex.

As soon as they had settled in, Nora wrote to her mother and sister Kathleen to come and visit them. Her mother declined because of age, but Kathleen was delighted. Her uncle Michael Healy generously financed the visit. Kathleen arrived at Euston at 5 a.m. and there was no one to meet her. "She cried like the rain" and was much relieved when

104

the Joyces arrived at the station.

Kathleen and Joyce always got on well. Kathleen was full of fun and outspoken and Joyce admired these qualities. They often went on long walks together and Kathleen talked about Galway and the people and places he knew there. Joyce was fascinated with her turn of phrase and was prepared to honour her principles and humour her fancies. He even took her to Mass on Sunday saying "you know what they'll be saying at home if I don't".

Kathleen was a god-send to the Joyces as she brought a spark of normality into their lives with her banter. She found "Nora all go and Jim all stand still", and Nora whispered to her in confidence that Joyce was "a weakling.. I always have to be after his tail... I wish I were married to a man like my father".

Early in August, Kathleen returned to Galway, loaded with presents for her mother and family. Mrs. Donnellan, her next door neighbour in Bowling Green, well remembers her return. She had left in June dressed in the simple clothes of an ordinary Galway girl of the time and she returned "done up to the knocker" dressed in "the finery of Paris and wearing make-up", something then unknown in Galway. She was the envy of every girl of Galway as, from that day forward, parcel after parcel of the most up to date fashions arrived in Bowling Green.

The 1920s were to be punctuated by eye operations for Joyce. He was also busy writing *Finnegan's Wake*, a labour that was long and exhausting. Adverse criticism of the book hurt him deeply and resulted in severe depression and nervous anxieties. Through all of this, Nora was his constant nurse and companion. During 1927, Joyce's old friend John Francis Byrne called on them in Paris. Joyce and he had not met since 1909, and they had many things to discuss. Nora too found Byrne honest and fortright. She opened up her soul to him and asked him to intercede with Joyce and validate their marriage. Byrne found Joyce willing to validate their common law marriage. He presumed that they would do so straight away, but for some reason the

105

matter was dropped and the marriage was not then celebrated.

A year later Nora complained of not feeling well. It was suspected she had cancer and an operation was recommended. In his great grief at her illness and as proof positive of his deep love for Nora, Joyce insisted on staying with her in the American hospital. A bed was fixed up for him in her room and there he stayed.

Nora was operated on in November 1928 and was given radium treatment, but her complaint lived on and she remained sickly. She had to return to hospital the following February for a hysterectomy and again, Joyce took a bed beside her in the hospital. He stayed there until Nora was given the all-clear, sometime towards the end of March. Speaking of this, Richard Ellmann says, "He depended upon Nora to hold his life together by her loyalty and by her contempt for his weaknesses. There was no one else to whom he spoke without deliberation."

The Joyce home was now the meeting place of Joyce's many literary friends and Nora had to cater for them. International figures jostled one another in their simple apartment. Adrienne Monnier, Paul Leopold Leon and his wife Lucie, Herbert Gorman, Samuel Beckett, Eugene Jolas, Ivan Goll, Philippe Soupault, Louis Gillet, Sylvia Beach, Padraic and Mary Colum were amongst the constant callers. Nora liked the visitors, liked their company when she was forewarned of their coming and was prepared for them; but like any housewife she resented being caught unprepared and was never slow to show Joyce that she was not to be taken for granted.

In 1931, the Joyces moved to London with the idea of staying there indefinitely and there, their marriage was finally legalised. Joyce chose his father's brithday, July 4th, as his wedding day.

In accordance with English law, Joyce had to insert a notice of intent to marry a month before the event. This notice did not name the day or date of the marriage but it was sufficient to alert the press and public about the coming event.

The Joyces duly arrived at the Registry Office on the 4th of July. Joyce declared that Nora and he had already been married but that Nora, with Joyce's connivance, had been married under the name of Gretta Greene. The registrar, on hearing this, pronounced that they could not marry a second time unless they were first divorced. But Joyce's solicitor pointed out that in English law the first marriage was invalid and void because the husband was party to Nora assuming a fictitious name. The registrar accepted this and performed the ceremony.

The entry in the Registry Office reads:-

"James Augustus Joyce, aged 49, Bachelor. Independent means, married Nora Joseph Barnacle, Spinster, aged 47, each then residing at 28B Cambden Grove, London, W. 8 on 4th July 1931"

As they left the Registry Office, they were surrounded by press reporters and photographers. The next day, the *Evening Standard* featured the wedding with a front page heading and photograph. The news of the wedding raised many eyebrows but it caused utter consternation in Galway particularly amongst neighbours of the Barnacle family in Bowling Green.

One of these neighbours, Mrs. Donnellan, clearly recalls the reaction of Nora's mother when confronted with a copy of the newspaper. She was furious and threatened legal action on anyone who would dare suggest that the Joyces weren't married in 1904. She insisted that the event in London was due to the fact that their original marriage certificate could not be traced in Trieste because of the ravages of war in that city. But tongues wagged in that close community and the neighbours placed more store in the newspaper story than they did in the explanations offered by the Barnacles.

Kathleen Barnacle was immediately despatched to London to sort out the facts. During her previous visit, Joyce had given her a present of a watch and the first thing he noticed

107

was she wasn't wearing it. When he questioned her about it, she told him she had pawned it! "Just what I'd do myself" he told her laughing at her embarrassment.

As before, Joyce and Kathleen got on very well together, touring London and its neighbourhood. Nora, too, was delighted with her sister's visit as she now had a relative to whom she could pour out her soul. She had been sick and tired of the life they had in Paris. No privacy, no home life. She was weary of sitting with and listening to artists until the wee hours of the morning. Not that she in any way contemplated leaving Joyce. They had soldiered far too long together. There were his illnesses and his eyes to be nursed. He was a hopeless manager and had no idea of how to handle money. At their ages sex was far less important than deep friendship and, despite their ordinary tiffs, their marriage was firmly based on the solid rocks of compatibility and temperament.

The story of their marriage to be brought home by Kathleen was a rehash of the story that their first marriage was void and invalid in English law because of a mix-up in Trieste. Nora's mother was very happy with this explanation and, in her positive way, she undid the effect of the previous rumours.

Life in England did not suit the Joyces and they returned to Paris where they lived for most of the next ten years. Joyce worked hard at the completion of *Finnegan's Wake*, but he suffered periodic bouts of illness. Lucia's mental illness became more pronounced, and she was finally committed to a home in 1935. Giorgio's marriage was also a source of anxiety and his wife, Helen, suffered a number of mental breakdowns.

Through all of this, Nora was the crutch on which the whole family leaned. Many contemporaries noted her devotion to Joyce and his dependence on her. Lucie Noel, wife of Paul Leon, speaking of her in 1940, had this to say of her:-

> "It must be extremely hard to be the wife of a great man in any case, but to be the wife of a

semi blind writer must be doubly difficult. I can say in all sincerity that I do not believe James Joyce could have coped with the difficulties of daily life had it not been for the great devotion and courage of his wife Nora. Their's was a constant companionship based on love and congenial understanding. Anyone who knew Mr. and Mrs. Joyce realized that no important move could be made one without the other. Unless one had seen them together one would not realize how much James Joyce depended on his wife Nora. In all the blows that fate dealt Joyce and his family, through all the trials and tribulations, they remained devotedly together".

(Lucie Noel:- James Joyce and Paul L. Leon:
The Story of a Friendship, The Gotham Book
Mart, New York, 1950. pp. 30-31).

World War 11 forced the Joyces to return to Switzerland. Joyce was very ill and Nora was worried about him. She confided her fears as to his health to Jacques Mercanton the journalist who had become friendly with the Joyces:-

"Mrs Joyce confided to me her constant worries
about his health. He ate poorly, and less and less;
there had been days when he was so exhausted
she thought she would lose him".

(Portraits of the Artist in Exile,
Wolfhound Press, P. 252.)

Nora also told Mercanton how gay they had been in Paris before all their troubles. In the same passage, Nora shows her spirit as well as her devoted love for Joyce:-

"I joined Mrs. Joyce at Mass, and then we went
to the hotel together. On the way, she told me
in her charming manner about their life in Paris,
so tiring when Joyce, more out of nervousness
than for the pleasure of it, insisted on going out
to dine in a restaurant every night.

"I have put up with him for thirty-four years",
she said on a note of mocking tenderness that

109

corresponded exactly to his "I deserve some credit, don't you think?"
It was a credit she had no intention of foregoing, to judge from the solicitous question she put to me about Jim's frame of mind, his rest, the good he was doing himself with this stay in Switzerland."

(Portraits of the Artist in Exile,
Wolfhound Press, P. 233).

In one other passage, Nora reveals the permanency of her love for Joyce, and how he had remained for her that "little boy" she had met in Dublin so many years before:-
"One evening, while we were waiting for him in the hotel lobby, Mrs. Joyce described Joyce to me as he was when she met him for the first time in Dublin, many years before: his expression strange and severe, an overcoat that hung down to his feet, shoes down at the heel, a big, white sombrero. She drew his portrait with tender irony, astonished that a long life together, every instant shared (for they were seldom apart) had not effaced that fleeting image. "He is old", she said gently, "but he has not changed much. In so many ways, he is a little boy, as you have noticed".
One sensed that, at the end of so many years, she still relied in full confidence on that "little boy" and asked for nothing better".

(Portraits of an Artist in Exile,
Wolfhound Press, p. 238)

The Joyces moved to Zurich on the 17th December 1940. Joyce was now a very sick man and was slow to visit any of his many friends. He spoke often of death and seemed to be absorbed by it. Despite all this, they had a convivial Christmas. They had dinner with friends and afterwards sang Irish songs and even Latin hymns.

On the 10th January 1941, Joyce was overcome by violent stomach pains. On the following day, he was taken to the Red Cross hospital and was X-rayed. It was discovered he had a perforated ulcer. He dreaded an operation as he was utterly afraid of losing consciousness. His son Giorgio talked him into having one, but not without difficulty.

The operation seemed very successful but soon he had a bad turn. He passed into a coma. When he awoke for a moment he asked that Nora sleep beside him as he had done when she was in hospital. The doctors urged Nora to go home.

Joyce lapsed into a coma again, and on the morning of the 13th January 1941 at 2.15 a.m., he died before Nora could reach his bedside.

Two days later Joyce was buried in the Fluntern cemetery. A Catholic priest offered to conduct a religious service at the graveside but Nora, while appreciating the offer, said "I couldn't do that to him". Nora's wreath on the coffin was in the form of a harp. She had it made that way, as she was to tell a friend "for my Jim, because he loved music so much".

The Zurich art critic Dr. Carola Giedion-Welcker was at the funeral and described Nora's poignant farewell to her husband:-

> "However the most striking part of the ceremony came at the end when Nora Joyce had to part from the lowering coffin and with a simple, impulsive gesture spread out her arms for a farewell, while she bent lovingly over the wooden coffin as though to prevent the final lowering".
>
> *(Portraits of the Artist in Exile,*
> Wolfhound Press, p. 279).

Following Joyce's death, Nora lived on in Zurich. She had no income other than from the royalties from Joyce's books and the generosity of some freinds. World War 11 was at its height and it was difficult for her to receive the royalties, so she knew poverty once more. Joyce's death was a great wrench in her life. She put it very succintly when she said "things are very dull now, there was always

111

something doing when he was about".

Her contacts with Galway were now broken. Her eldest sister Mary had married William Blackmore, a native of Galway city. He was in the army and contemplating deserting to America to join the Blackmore family there. Michael Healy wouldn't allow this and he bought William out of the army so he could emigrate legally with his head held high. So Mary was in the U.S.A. in 1941.

Her sister Delia (Bridget) went to the U.S.A. also: out to a girl friend she had known in Galway. She spent four years in exile there but was forced by ill-health to return to her native air. Shortly afterwards she had a rather severe nervous breakdown and was a patient for a while in the mental hospital in Ballinasloe. She never recovered full health. She never married though she had many suitors. She was dead in 1941. Nora's third sister, Margaret, had emigrated during World War 1 to England. She worked in hotels in London and gradually lost touch with her family in Galway. She seldom wrote home and, as she changed work quite often, her whereabouts were never clearly known. Indeed Kathleen Barnacle failed to find any trace of her when she came to London to visit the Joyces. It is almost certain that she died unmarried. That she did so was vouched for by Margaret Moore a nonogenerian Galway woman living in Market Drayton, Shropshire. She was a close friend of the Barnacles and kept in touch with them down the years.

Margaret's twin sister was Annie. She emigrated to the U.S.A. to her sister Mary Blackmore. Here she was a maid governess to a fairly wealthy family, who lived close to the Blackmores. She visited her sister regularly. She contracted the flu in 1918 and died. Annie never married.

Nora's only brother Thomas worked as a conductor on the old horse drawn trams that plied between Galway and Salthill. When the trams gave way to buses, he retained his job. But one day he disappeared and soon the news broke that he had eloped to England with a nice girl. He never wrote home. His mother heard from others who met him that he had a good job in England. He lived on to the fifties and is buried in England. It is not known whether he had any children. If he had they are the last surviving Barnacles, a family that contributed so much to Galway life for two centuries.

Nora's youngest sister Kathleen remained on with her mother at 4 Bowling Green (now No. 8). After her mother's death in 1940, she remained there with her husband. She had married John Griffin of Middle Street Galway in 1937. She had the figure, colouring and flair of Nora. It was extraordinary that, of all the Barnacle family, Kathleen was the closest to the Joyces. She was only eight years old when Nora left Galway. Perhaps the fact that she was the only Barnacle to remain in Galway had something to do with it.

Kathleen worked as a bookbinder in O'Gormans and later in the Connacht Tribune. It is probable that Nora worked part time as a binder in O'Gormans before she left Galway. She would have learned the trade in the Convent of Mercy and O'Gormans often took on casual staff when very busy. While there is no actual record of Nora being there, she is remembered as having worked in the bookbindery. This is reinforced by the fact that Joyce sent an inscribed copy of *Ulysses* to O'Gormans when it was published.

Kathleen was highly strung and on occasions threw tantrums. When she married in 1937, she was 42, and would have been regarded as being past child bearing age. But for her own good reasons, Kathleen thought different. Soon after she married, she announced she was pregnant and began wearing maternity clothes. However, it soon became clear she was suffering from imaginitis and she became the laughing stock of Galway. To escape further humiliation, Kathleen and her husband betook themselves to London where John had no difficulty in getting work. He was a highly skilled French polisher. They lived in London until the sixties and then poor Kathleen developed leukaemia. She had a most painful last few years and died in agony.

Thus in 1941, Nora had no choice but to remain in Zurich. Her friends and family had all left Galway and with World War 11, there was no chance of leaving Switzerland.

Life was not at all easy for her. She suffered a great deal from arthritis. After the war she travelled around the haunts of other days. She visited Paris and Vichy and her daughter Lucia who was still in hospital. Her son Giorgio visited her and her grandson Stephen often spent holiday periods with her in Zurich.

There is some evidence that Nora was still practising her religion. We have already noted how Jacques Mercanton walked with her from Sunday Mass to the hotel in Lausanne just before Joyce's death. Her grandson Stephen recalls that, whenever he visited his granny, she insisted on taking him to Mass with her, often against his will.

This suggests that Nora became reconciled with her church and, with the loneliness and pain that followed Joyce's death, sought consolation and perhaps peace in the religion of her forefathers. While pleasant enough, thanks to the generosity and concern of her many friends there, life in Zurich was lonely for Nora. Lucia's illness was a blow she still found very hard to come to terms with. Giorgio's visits brought solace and comfort, but only for a time.

When, after the war, the body of W.B. Yeats was brought home to be buried near Ben Bulben, Nora asked the Irish Government to do Joyce the honour of removing his remains to Ireland. Her request was ignored. Nora felt this refusal keenly. She became all the more bitter towards Ireland when she was told that Yeats' remains landed at the docks of her native Galway and were conveyed through the city in triumph.

A result of her bitterness towards Ireland was that she prevented Harriet Weaver, Joyce's great benefactor, from donating the manuscript of *Finnegan's Wake* to the National Library. Instead she sent it to the British Museum, an act which Joyce would have applauded.

Nora's health began to fail. She suffered severely from arthritis which gradually worsened, leaving her in 1950 practically immobile. She was taking ever increasing doses of cortisone. Her system finally reacted to this and she contracted uremic poisoning. Towards the end of March

1951, at the age of 67, her health finally failed. She was removed to the convent hospital in Zurich for further treatment. The Catholic chaplain visited her, and there is no way of knowing what went on during these visits. One would have said that Nora was reconciled to her religion were it not that her son Giorgio is on record as saying that "she sent the priest away". This seems to contradict her grandson's memory of his holidays with her in Zurich.

Nora died in Zurich on April 10th 1951. She lies buried in the Fluntern cemetery but not in the same grave as Joyce. As was the Swiss custom, a panegyric was given at her graveside. The orator was a Catholic priest who, at one stage, referred to Nora as "a great sinner".

This statement may be out of context but it is undoubtedly harsh on the woman whose courage, loyalty and humour gave so much to world literature in that she was an essential part of Joyce and his art. Some thirty years before her death, Nora had known the artist Arthur Power. He became very close to the Nora in the Paris of the 1920s and later was to describe Joyce in the book *The Joyce we Knew*. This, perhaps, should have been her panegyric:-

> Nora, "this charming, natural woman always kind
> and friendly, and who through the troubled sea of
> married life from the darkness of obscurity to
> the high-light of fame had always managed to
> hold her family together with her courage and her
> rock-firm common sense. It is true that she was
> not an intellectual in any sense; and why should
> she be? But nevertheless she was a sincere and
> gallant woman, and his worthy companion and
> mate — this breath of Galway air in the
> intellectual hot-house of Paris".